FBI

INSIDE USA'S NATIONAL INTELLIGENCE & SECURITY

FBI

INSIDE USA'S NATIONAL INTELLIGENCE & SECURITY

N. CHOKKAN

PRABHAT
PRAKASHAN

Published by
PRABHAT PRAKASHAN PVT. LTD.
4/19 Asaf Ali Road,
New Delhi-110 002 (INDIA)
e-mail: prabhatbooks@gmail.com

ISBN 978-93-5562-339-3

FBI – INSIDE USA'S NATIONAL INTELLIGENCE & SECURITY
by N. Chokkan

Edition
First, 2024

Price
₹ 300 (Rupees Three Hundred Only)

Printed at
Sita Fine Arts, Delhi

Author's Note

In the shadows of American history, the Federal Bureau of Investigation (FBI) stands as a formidable force, celebrated for its triumphs in tracking down criminals, thwarting espionage, and combatting terrorism on a global scale. For nearly a century, the FBI has cultivated a legendary aura, weaving tales of its successes into the fabric of American law enforcement.

The aim of this book is to delve beneath the surface, beyond the polished image meticulously crafted by the agency, and to expose a less idealized and more real vision of the FBI. Established in 1908 with a modest staff of three dozen, the FBI has transformed into a vast organization of over 27,000 agents and support personnel. Throughout its evolution, the agency's role has shifted significantly from traditional law enforcement to intelligence operations. This transformation prompts us to examine the consequences of such a shift for the democratic fabric of our nation.

As we navigate through the pages that follow, we will confront the inherent tension between the FBI's quest for absolute secrecy and the foundational principles of civil liberties and agency accountability. The stories within will peel back the layers of secrecy, revealing covert operations and hidden agendas that challenge our conventional understanding of the FBI's mission.

While the FBI's successes have rightfully earned admiration, a closer examination is necessary to comprehend the price paid for these achievements. This book seeks to shed light on the complexities and controversies that have accompanied the FBI's journey from its early days to the present. It invites readers to question assumptions, scrutinize narratives, and explore the intricate dance between power, secrecy, and the preservation of democratic values.

❑

Contents

Author's Note 5

1. G-Men 9
2. Secret Friends 21
3. Bureau 33
4. For Oil… 45
5. Action and Intelligence 55
6. Double Trouble 69
7. New Rival 78
8. Nuclear Bomb, Weapon and Danger 88
9. True or False 102
10. Before and After Hoover 107
11. Wall 120
12. The Cat and Mouse Chase 128

References 133

1
G-Men

It was Saturday 22nd July 1933 ,close to midnight. It was a small room which was quite dark. The centre of the room was dimly lit. Four people ,two men and their wives were playing bridge—. They were one of the wealthiest people in Oklahoma. There was a lavish amount of food and drinks on a table near them.

It was around 11:15 p.m. A door of the room was cracked open. They did not consider it amiss, and so they did not drop their cards and continued with their game.

The intruders approached the table and aimed their guns at them.

"Hey, who are you? How did you come here?" one of the men shouted and tried to get up.

The intruder replied "No one should utter a sound. Stay quiet. Else, be ready to face the consequences."

There was pin drop silence for the next few minutes. Then they pointed at the two men and asked, "Who is Urschel between the two of you?"

Their eyes was full of fear, the women looked at them and were terrified at the way their husbands were taken away. Another kidnapper armed with a pistol approached on the females. "Until we leave, no one should move a muscle and if you try to call for any help then you will not see your husbands alive."

There was no answer to their question. They hesitated a while.

Then one intruder said, "If you don't tell us, we will be forced to take both of you"

Still, no answer.

"OK, now both of you get up!" the one with the gun ordered. "Raise your hands and walk out."

Their eyes was full of fear, the women looked at them and were terrified at the way their husbands were taken away. Another kidnapper armed with a pistol approached on the females. "Until we leave, no one should move a muscle and ifyou try to call for any help then you will not see your husbands alive."

They agreed, in fear. The armed man left and the door closed. After a few minutes, they heard a car leaving. Both women were clueless ,why did they kidnapped their husbands?

"What do we do now?"

"I don't know."

"They could have kidnapped them for money. Recently, the number of kidnappers targeting rich men for ransom has gone up."

The kidnappers had targeted on Charles Urschel. Unfortunately, Walter Jarett was also taken just because he was playing cards with Urschel. Fortunately, they did not make him suffer for long. When they identified Urschel, they released Jarett.

"What does this mean? Do we have to sit idly until they contact us for ransom?"

"Not necessary. I saw an advertisement that we must immediately inform the government about the kidnapping. We should call the number and convey that we are in trouble. They will help."

They quickly found the advertisement, called the number and explained the incident in detail.

"Thank you for the information, madam. We will start our investigation immediately and please share any updates you get with us."

"Sure."

Two men were kidnapped: Charles Urschel and Walter Jarrett.

The kidnappers had targeted on Charles Urschel. Unfortunately, Walter Jarett was also taken just because he was playing cards with Urschel. Fortunately, they did not make him suffer for long. When they identified Urschel, they released Jarett.

Jarett somehow reached home. He was concerned about the whereabouts of Urschel.

The federal officers conducted an intense investigation. They collected various information like the identities of the kidnappers, their way of communication, the car which they used, the direction they went, and more. However, they could not find the details of the kidnappers. Based on a lot of information and possible angles, they conducted their investigation.

> *While his eyes and ears were covered, he used his other senses to function more efficiently than before. What is the type of vehicle the kidnappers are using?Which road they are taking? Type of road? How long is the travel? Is there any special odour? Am I able to identify any other special clues about the route?*

At the same time, those who kidnapped Urschel had already travelled a long way. They planned to escape to a remote location before the government tracked them down. However, they failed to notice that Urschel, the victim was not nervousneither worried, nor screamed in anger or fear, nor begged them to let him go. He behaved as though he was going on a picnic with them and remained extremely composed.

Charles Urschel had earned a fortune in the oil industry. He was not just rich, but also smart and exceptionally brilliant. Even though he was blindfolded and his ears were covered , his senses were very sharp and his brain functioned efficiently. He did not really worry even after being kidnapped. He tried to make a mental map and remember how and where the kidnappers were taking him, accurately.

While his eyes and ears were covered, he used his other senses to function more efficiently than before. *What is the type of vehicle the kidnappers are using?Which road they are taking? Type of road? How long is the travel? Is there any special odour? Am I able to identify any other special clues about the route?*

By now, Urschel collected all the information about the room, the kidnappers and the place where he was locked for a few days. While he was blindfolded, he had gathered a lot of information by keeping his ears open. The kidnappers were unaware of it.

The kidnappers were not aware of the fact that Urschel was intensely trying to register these facts. After several hours of driving, he was locked in a small room. Later, he was shifted to another place.

Meanwhile, Urschel's family was given a warning letter via one of Urschel's friends demanding:

'If you want Mr. Urschel to be released alive, you must give us two hundred thousand US dollars.'

For Urschel family, two hundred thousand dollars was not a big deal of money. So, they were ready to pay the money and get him back. At the same time, the government had also appointed an agents to find the kidnappers. Since the news about the kidnapping was publicised in the newspapers and magazines, they got many pieces of evidence. Based on the clues, they were planning an operation to capture the real kidnappers.

Urschel's family was in a dilemma. They were in a predicament as to whether they should wait for the government to trace and rescue him or should they give the money as demanded by the kidnappers.

The government did not interfere in their decision. They advised, "In case if you decide to pay, tell us the numbers of the dollar notes."

"Why?"

"After you give us the details, we may be able to accurately find out the whereabouts of the kidnappers by tracing where those dollars are being spent."

After that, Urschel's family did not delay further. They arranged the money demanded by the kidnappers. The money was exchanged in the way that you would have read about in many crime novels.

After some time, in another corner of the US, the room in which Urschel was held was unlocked. "Mr. Urschel, you are now free. You can go immediately."

Urschel asked from them ,"Why? Have your demands been met?"

But they did not respond him. However, Urschel understood the circumstances. As usual, he left without any arguments. By now , Urschel collected all the information about the room, the kidnappers and the place where he was locked for a few days. While he was blindfolded, he had gathered a lot of information by keeping his ears open. The kidnappers were unaware of it.

As they got their money and so released him happily. They gave Urschel ten dollars from Urschel's money and asked him to travel back safely to his home. Urschel reached home. He embraced and consoled his beloved family members who were relieved to see him safe and sound. He rested well after his arduous experience. Very soon, he decided to speak to the government officials.

"Yes, Mr. Urschel, were you able to identify your kidnappers? Why did they kidnap you? Do you have any information about it?"

Urschel told them all the details he had managed to observe while he was kidnapped. The government officials were astounded when he narrated the exact information as if describing the screenplay of a thriller movie.

"Mr. Urschel, you are unbelievable. It is really startling that you managed to collect a lot of information, amidst the trauma."

"Hold your reactions! Try to trace them based on the details I have provided."

The government had already progressed a lot in finding the kidnappers. With many clues, and solid pieces of evidence in Urschel's kidnapping, they (correctly) predicted that the kidnapper was 'Machine Gun Kelly'.

Who is 'Machine Gun Kelly'? Is he like 'Billy the Kid', and 'Calamity Jane'?

The real name of Machine Gun Kelly was 'George Kelly Barnes'. He was typical local robber. His wife Katherine bought him a gun and motivated him to become an eminent burglar. Later, he was known as Machine Gun Kelly in his circle of rowdies.

There are many interesting stories revolve around Kelly's machine gun. He was known for firing a barrage on a wall with this machine gun, which is one of those stories. When you check out the wall, you could see the word 'Kelly' in the pattern made by the gunshots. All these stories are good to hear.

In fact, Kelly was not such a thug as described in the stories. He carried the machine gun only because his wife had gifted him.But he had never shot anyone.

There are many interesting stories revolve around Kelly's machine gun. He was known for firing a barrage on a wall with this machine gun, which is one of those stories. When you check out the wall, you could see the word 'Kelly' in the pattern made by the gunshots. All these stories are good to hear.

In those times, the entire country had a lot of hooligans like Kelly. Thousands of innocent people were affected by many small, medium, and big burglaries, robbery, and kidnapping activities.

Due to this, the federal government decided to keep their country free of crimes. The government mad e swift and intense efforts to track those who were unruly in the respective regions and prosecute them. Yet, Kelly managed to get away from the hands of the government,even though Kelly was s suspected in many cases but there was no sufficient evidence against him.

Before marrying Katherine, Kelly was a-run-of-the-mill thug, and a bootlegger. He was caught and put into jail quite a few times. Surprisingly, he transformed after his marriage. Reports say that his wife Katherine told him a lot of motivational stories which led to his transformation into a bigger criminal. So, apart from smuggling alcohol, he also indulged in other criminal activities like bank robbery and kidnapping, and extorting money. Kidnapping Urschel and extorting two hundred thousand dollars from his family was his biggest accomplishment.

Based on the clues provided by Kelly, the government officers identified the whereabouts of the place he was held captive. After that, investigation progressed, finding whether anyone was associated with Urschel in those localities. They got solid evidence like winning a lottery. "Kelly's mother-in-law lives here. His brother-in-law runs a farm here!"

On the other hand, Urschel didn't plan to let him get away scot-free. Based on the clues provided by Kelly, the government officers identified the whereabouts of the place he was held captive. After that, investigation progressed , finding whether anyone was associated with Urschel in those localities. They got solid evidence like winning a lottery. "Kelly's mother-in-law lives here. His brother-in-law runs a farm here!"

Immediately, the government officials flew to that locality. They arrived at the location and searched for pieces of evidence. All the clues of identification provided by Urschel they were accurately matched. What else did they need? The police encircled both Kelly's mother-in-law's home and brother-in-law's farm. The information leaked out soon upon the arrest and interrogation of the people in that locality.

Apart from that, the police had already noted the numbers of the bills of the extortion money given to Kelly. Eventually, they also started receiving information from the places where the bills were spent. Based on that information, it became easy for them to find out the criminals involved in this kidnapping activity.

In the next few days, many people who were involved in kidnapping Urschel were arrested. Everyone pointed towards Machine Gun Kelly. It was revealed that another person named Albert Bates partnered with him. Very soon he was caught. But the question is where was Kelly? Where was his wife? It remained a mystery.

Upon the continuous arrest of Kelly's partners who were involved in the crime, the Urschel family received a threatening letter stating that, "Stop hunting for us.We are not responsible for the severe consequences!"

Earlier, when Urschel was held by Kelly, the government officials conducted secret investigations. Since he was given security, they did not bother with these threats. Gradually, they were closing in around Kelly.

It had been exactly two months since Urschel was kidnapped. At the end of September 1933, they got new evidence. "Kelly and his wife are hiding at Memphis. They are being sheltered by a man named Tichenor." The next day, a special force reached Memphis. They surrounded the home suspected to be Kelly's hideout.

No one had ever had a conversation with him or become close to him after his transformation from a petty thief to a big-time criminal. In fact, they were anxious over the number of stories they had heard about his machine gun and clueless as to how he might react.

Turned out, they could have remained as cool as a cucumber. Their early morning attack ended up in an anti-climax. When the government officials forced an entry, they couldn't find even a toy gun in Kelly's hand!

On the other hand, it seemed, Kelly was expecting their arrival. When policemen surrounded him, he raised his hands and requested, "Don't shoot, G-Men."

What is G-Men?

G means the government.. G-men mean people who work on behalf of the government.

Before that, the term 'G-Men' generally indicated all the government employees. However, after this Machine Gun Kelly incident, it has become a special term dedicated exclusively for the specific department that investigated and arrested him.

In fact, some stated that Kelly did not utter a word during the raid in the wee hours. A few others gave a different statement that Kelly's wife named the government officials as 'G-Men'. However, there are other claims that 'both the statements are fake; it is just a story cooked up by the journalists'.

We are not sure which is true. However, today G-Men invariably refer to the FBI. They have captured and dealt with relatively more dangerous and smart criminals than Machine Gun Kelly. Yet, the honour earned by the Federal Bureau of Investigation remains intact. "It's even difficult to imagine the world without G-Men," admit many.

Who are these G-Men? From where did they come? What do they do? What are their powers and rights? How do they work? Are they capable enough to receive the special tag as G-Men like Superman? Why do we think of the CIA when it comes to American Intelligence? What is the difference between the FBI and CIA?

If you need explanations to all these, our story needs to travel back before 1933. In fact, we need to take a trip before at least a quarter-century.

Guess what, even that's not enough. Let's travel back even further. We can clearly understand the story during the end of the American Civil War in 1865. Shall we?

❑

2
Secret Friends

During the middle of the 19th century ,the US, the world's leader was once caught intensely in a tug of war situation. They had no external rivals, but the provinces fought with each other resisting harmonisation. They threatened that 'if you force, we will form a new country'.

The cause of concern was , Should the US abolish slavery or not!

During that period, only a few states in the US had agreed to eradicate the practice of slavery. Others refused to abolish it. There were few more confused groups, unable to make a choice.

During the 1860 election in the US, the practice of slavery was a significant issue to be addressed. The citizens were eager to know whether the president would support the slaves or be the representative of the rich men.

> *The US witnessed the commencement of the Civil War in the year 1861. Under the leadership of Abraham Lincoln provinces that eradicated the practice of slavery and provinces in the border, joined hands. They battled against the Southern States.*

In that election, Abraham Lincoln contested on behalf of the Republican Party. Many believed that if Lincoln won the election, he would put an end to the miserable slave lives of millions. This is the major reason why the rich landlords (in the Southern States) hated Lincoln. While they disregarded him with hate speech, on the other hand, they indulged in many secret activities to defeat Lincoln in the election. However, people favoured Lincoln. He won the election and became the new president.

Eventually, the Southern States became uptight. Fearing that Lincoln might take full control over them, they immediately announced, "We are no longer part of the US. We are setting up a new government."

Abraham Lincoln refused to recognise it. He strongly disapproved, stating, "It is essential to improve the lives of slaves. However, I will never allow America to be divided into pieces."

The landlords of the Southern States did not listen to him. They created a name among themselves and elected a president. "Lincoln, Who's that?" was their mortifying tone. In this chaotic circumstance, Lincoln had no option other than harnessing the power of the military to get things under control.

Some rich landlords indulged in human trafficking. The upper-class population seduced and kidnapped innocent women and sold them. Poor people smuggled liquor. They illegally cut the trees in the forest and sold them. They printed fake currency notes.

The US witnessed the commencement of the Civil War in the year 1861. Under the leadership of Abraham Lincoln provinces that eradicated the practice of slavery and provinces in the border, joined hands. They battled against the Southern States. Since the opponents were strong and the counter-attack was powerful, the war continued for a long time. Many feared that the prolonged war might split the country into two.

The Civil War revealed many noble traits of Abraham Lincoln. Integrating different people and versatile groups, fighting for a common cause, imparting control and victory over the rivals are his historical achievements irrelevant to this book. In the year 1865, the American Civil War came to an end. Those who threatened the unity of America were restrained. After many months, America breathed in peace.

However, President Lincoln was restless. "We conquered this fight. What happens if it is likely to recur in other provinces and if they demand a separate country?"

He was constantly thinking that this may destroy the whole country. Whether the opposition was small or big, the president decided to put out the fire.

Although the civil war within the country ended, other crimes happened regularly. Some rich landlords indulged in human trafficking. The upper-class population seduced and kidnapped innocent women and sold them. Poor people smuggled liquor. They illegally cut the trees in the forest and sold them. They printed fake currency notes.

Who printed the counterfeit notes? How was it brought into the market for use? How would they find it? Nothing was clear. Everyone from common people, shopkeepers, industries and businesses were severely affected due to the fake currency.

After brainstorming a lot about the eradication of the counterfeiters, Abraham Lincoln zeroed in on a decision. "We need a secret mission force to handle and prevent big crimes that happen within the US."

Why? Already, every nook and corner of the US had police force. Weren't they sufficient enough to handle these crimes? Policemen were already burdened with a lot on their hands. They would collapse if this burden was added to their existing responsibilities.

The jurisdiction of the policemen was constrained to their respective localities. On the contrary, counterfeiters did not work as smaller groups. They were dangerous beyond the borders of the countries. They bought the paper from one country in the west, ink from a country from the east, printed in a southern country, and put it into use in a northern country. How would the police initiate legal proceedings?

The country was flooded with fake currency notes. Soon, another nation-wide concern may blossom. It was difficult to depend on the police force alone for these activities. A dedicated force made for a good call.

The US Secret Service created in the year 1865, is still running effectively ,almost 150 years. However, never in their service in all these years, did they sideline their goals and responsibilities. "We are not for publicity. Let's do our duty. It is more than enough.

On 5th July 1865, the first US Secret Service was incorporated. Unfortunately, Abraham Lincoln never had the chance to witness it. On 15th April ,he was shot dead just a few months ago The Secret Service department precisely termed as SS, was initially involved in the investigation and dealing of counterfeiters. Later, it started detecting other crimes like murder, burglary, gambling, etc.

At the same time, the public was kept uninformed about the Secret Service. The government had completely hidden the fact about the existence and functioning of a secret detective force from the eyes and ears of the public. Obviously, the Secret Service agents would be able to perform their jobs without any disturbances.

The US Secret Service created in the year 1865, is still running effectively, almost 150 years. However, never in their service in all these years, did they sideline their goals and responsibilities. "We are not for publicity. Let's do our duty. It is more than enough."

Indeed, it is an interesting job to work as undercover agents. If they did not exist, a lot of criminals would have split America into pieces and questioned their existence.

Without causing a shadow of a doubt, the undercover agents were so supremely talented that they acted and investigated responsibly, collected all the pieces of evidence, and arrested the respective criminals.

> *He was not a particularly beloved or powerful leader. However, his unexpected death affected everyone. People were fuming. "The country is not safe even for the president." This incident provided an additional responsibility to the Secret Service agents.*

Hence, if the government department encountered any case or incongruity, they immediately called the undercover agents' and ask them to investigate the case.

"We are in. But it will cost! Are you okay with that?"

Do not be mistaken. This is not bribery or unaccounted income. The government departments must pay to hire the services of the secret agents. Agents use this money to travel from one place to another, pay for food and shelter, and their other expenditures.

Comparing to the other departments of the federal government, the expenses of Secret Services are on the higher side. Since their service was so crucial, the government paid without any negotiation. Gradually, all the government departments faced the situation that they must rely on the undercover agents. The graph of the secret agencies slowly paced in the authoritative arena of the US.

In the year 1897,'William McKinley' took charge as the president of the US. Towards the end of his official term of four years, he was killed in 1901.

He was not a particularly beloved or powerful leader. However, his unexpected death affected everyone. People were fuming. “The country is not safe even for the president.” This incident provided an additional responsibility to the Secret Service agents. “It is your responsibility to provide security to the American president.”

Regardless of any case that was likely to affect the public interest, he would immediately attend it. Charles Bonaparte would never hesitate to defend the public even if the opposing party was affluent and authoritative. He was daring and bold in his arguments.

To date, the American Secret Service have rendered their flawless and meticulous service. These special agents protect the president who currently serves the office, the vice president, and former ones, and their families.

After the death of William McKinley , ‘Theodore Roosevelt’ took charge as the president. He ruled the country for the next eight years. He was the one who offered a new and stronger outlook to the US.

Theodore Roosevelt had a close pal named General Charles Bonaparte. Looks like you could recall the name, Bonaparte.

It reminds us about the French emperor, warrior of the kings, Napoleon. This Charles Bonaparte was the grandson of Napoleon Bonaparte. Charles was an intelligent student and studied in reputed educational institutions like Harvard and Cambridge. He moved to America and started practicing as a lawyer.

Charles already had heaps of money, more than generations ever need. Hence, he did not consider his legal profession as a source of income. Rather, he focused on various social activities and the welfare of civilians.

It was the latter part of the 19th century. Regardless of any case that was likely to affect the public interest, he would immediately attend it. Charles Bonaparte would never hesitate to defend the public even if the opposing party was affluent and authoritative. He was daring and bold in his arguments.

Not just in the court, but he continued to voice his opinions in the public stage too. People were surprised by the fact that though he was born into a royal family, he defended the civilians.

During that time, Theodore Roosevelt held an important position in the government. Someone had told him about Charles Bonaparte. Since Roosevelt was a progressive ruler, he developed great respect and honour for Bonaparte even before seeing him in person.

In the year 1889, both Roosevelt and Charles were invited to speak in an event planned at Baltimore. It was the first time they met. Their friendship continued till their last days. In fact, throughout the country, civilians had a disgraceful opinion of the government officials. People mocked the government stating, "If you have money and recommendation, you can easily get a government job. Who cares for talent?" In fact, it was true in a sense.

Yet, Roosevelt did not buy into those recommendations. He was extra cautious to avoid these kinds of mishaps in the departments he was accountable for.

Although Charles was teasing, Roosevelt understood the concern behind it. He immediately thought that the American government must use this kind of talented, progressive, and thoughtful personality.

After exchanging the usual pleasantries upon their first meeting, Theodore Roosevelt and Charles discussed the concerns related to job recommendations, hiring talents, and more. Roosevelt was sure that the government departments give preference to talent.

"How sure are you?"

"Even recently, we were about to hire some armed men. We interviewed everyone and they were assessed on skills directly. We asked them to shoot at a marked target. We hired those who were spot on and ignored everyone else with the recommendations."

"No, instead of doing these, you should have tried something else," Charles said on a funny note. "You should have split the interviewees into groups of twos, asked them to shoot at each other, and appointed those who remained alive!"

Although Charles was teasing, Roosevelt understood the concern behind it. He immediately thought that the American government must use this kind of talented, progressive, and thoughtful personality.

In the next few years, Charles and Roosevelt became close friends. Almost during the same period, Roosevelt's political affluence grew exponentially. In the year 1901,he became the president of the US. Immediately, he called his best friend Charles Bonaparte. Roosevelt offered him some important responsibilities. However, it was not because of their friendship but because of his talent.

If the crime was not proven, the accused would easily escape using any loopholes from the hands of the law. That was the major reason, Roosevelt considered, the best lawyer, Charles Bonaparte would be the right person to appoint as the General Attorney. Looking at the severity of the punishments awarded to them, others must stay away from committing crimes.

In the year 1905, Charles Bonaparte became Secretary of the American Navy. In the subsequent year, he accepted the Attorney General's post along with Cabinet Status.

Compared to the other posts, the honour conferred by the Attorney General post made him extremely happy. He was elated that being an attorney himself, the position could help him utilise all his knowledge and skills. Considering the similar facts, Roosevelt appointed Charles as the Attorney General.

During those times, expropriating of lands was seemingly more. Affluent landlords were pillaging from the poor and innocent people. On the other hand, they were also ravaging the forests. There were also many other crimes like buying and selling people as slaves, sex trafficking, theft by forging a signature, and more.

It was not a difficult task to arrest the criminals. However, the difficult part was taking them to the court of law and charging them appropriately for their crime. If the crime was not proven, the accused would easily escape using any loopholes from the hands of the law. That was the major reason, Roosevelt considered, the best lawyer, Charles Bonaparte would be the right person to appoint as the General Attorney. Looking at the severity of the punishments awarded to them, others must stay away from committing crimes.

It was Charles Bonaparte's dream too! Based on his guidance, the legal department in the US worked most efficiently in a long time.

Just hold on! We started talking about Secret Services but went along a different path. How are these linked?

We have already seen that various federal departments used the service of undercover agents for different tasks. During the period when Charles was in charge, the legal department widely used the services of the secret agents.

For example, the department would receive a complaint about expropriating of land by landlords. It was not possible to arrest them immediately. An investigation must be called to identify whether the accusation was true or someone just cooked up a story out of hatred. The collection of appropriate pieces of evidence is essential. Otherwise, the case may fail in court.

At this juncture, Charles needed assistance from Secret Service agents. In all the important cases, the investigation and evidence provided by the undercover agents were used as evidence in the court and the criminals were punished appropriately.

How long could the government depend on others? The expenses were mounting to pay for the services of these agents. So, why don't we hire our own detectives?

The federal government ignored this recommendation. They strictly decided, "We cannot appoint different detective groups for different departments. Let us go with the existing Secret Service agents."

"We agree, Sir. Yet, it is really expensive to hire them."

"Doesn't matter. We have allocated a separate budget for them. Use the fund, and no more talk about setting up new departments."

The request for a new detective service was not raised. However, everyone was aware that it wouldn't last for a long time. An exclusive detective force was essential for the legal department. Even it was not an immediate need, it was needed sooner or later.

❑

3
Bureau

David Caldwell was a young attorney, worked in the office of the American Attorney General was a very active person and appeared in the court directly in many important cases.

Just like any other attorney in the Department of Justice, David Caldwell also hired the services of the secret agents in many cases. Despite the fact that it was expensive, he was extremely satisfied with the thoroughness of their work.

At the same time, Caldwell was rather irritated at an aspect. However much the secret undercover agents excelled at their work, they were not bound to be under the control of the Department of Justice. How was it possible to make the most of the services of those who were controlled by a different authority?

There was yet another problem. The Department of Justice did not have the rights or authority to appoint any specific agent to investigate a specific task. 'We need an undercover agent to investigate the task' was the common request given to the Department of Treasury. Theyin turn, assigned the agent who was free to take up a new task.

A long time ago, when the agency was set up, the first investigation task assigned to the Secret Service forcewas nothing but to investigating and arresting the criminals who involved in printing fake currency notes. All these come under the 'treasury' department. That is why the Secret Service was established.

What is the relation between the treasury and undercover agents?

A long time ago, when the agency was set up, the first investigation task assigned to the Secret Service forcewas nothing but to investigating and arresting the criminals who involved in printing fake currency notes. All these come under the 'treasury' department. That is why the Secret Service was established.

David Caldwell considered this as a major concern. "If we encounter a lot of cases tomorrow and if the situation demands a greater number of undercover agents, is it even possible to depend on the Secret Service agency? What if they cannot provide a sufficient number of agents for investigation? What is the consequence that we may encounter due to delay from them? We are accountable to answer the public and the government, isn't it?"

The office of the Attorney General understood the fairness in Caldwell's concerns. However, no one was aware of how to change the protocols.

At that time, Stanley Finch served in the accounting section of the Department of Justice. He also repeatedly said, "We need our own undercover agency."

Very soon, these concerns reached Attorney General Charles Bonaparte. He also considered this as a genuine request. He highlighted it in the annual report he submitted to the federal government.

"Currently, the Department of Justice is addressing many small and big cases. Yet, we do have any undercover agents or investigating specialists in our control. Hence, we are using the agents from the Department of Treasury to meet our investigative needs. There is no doubt that they are extreme professionals in their field.

"At the same time, the number of cases under our authority is mounting every day. Even in emergency investigation cases, we are dependent on the Department of Treasury, while we hang around until the appointment of the agent. Apparently, this delay may lead to major problems soon.

"So, if you can allow us to have an exclusive intelligence department, we can save a lot of money, execute our investigation with enhanced independence, and more effectivity. If you are unable to amend this immediately, it may indicate we are undermining the power of our Department of Justice."

Even after the recommendation and strong insistence made by the Attorney General, the government was not hasty. To verify the truth in his statements, the government called him for an investigation on 17th January 1908, asking "What is your exact problem?"

"We face a lot of difficulties in handling the undercover agents from the treasury. For example, their daily allowance is 3 dollars. It is now increased to 4 dollars. It increases our expenses too."

Even after the recommendation and strong insistence made by the Attorney General, the government was not hasty. To verify the truth in his statements, the government called him for an investigation on 17th January 1908 ,asking "What is your exact problem?"

"But this is not a major spend, right?"

"When you look at it individually, it is not a major expense. However, when you consider it collectively, even for trivial tasks, we have to plead with them, request for the agents, wait until their arrival, wait for their investigation reports and pieces of evidence, and all these things are likely to burden us. Despite all these strenuous efforts, we cannot question them even if the report has any discrepancy, because Department of Treasury is the only authority that can control them."

"Okay. Why don't you hire the services of private detective services instead?"

"Even that is not possible because different cases occur at different places. We are not sure if we can find skillful agents in the respective places. Even if we can find them, the basis of trust becomes questionable. What if they disclose the government secrets? If they falsify the investigation or take bribes, we cannot control them."

"Then, what do you propose as a solution to this problem?"

"There is only one solution. The Department of Justice must have its own secret agents, ready to deploy anytime. Even a small group is sufficient. We can manage them properly and meet our needs."

"Okay, we'll think about it!"

This time, the government really considered their request. *Can we assign an exclusive undercover agent department for the Department of Justice? Can we meet all the expenses? Is it possible to handle the additional expenses that may arise? Is it worth making a team?*

This time, the government really considered their request. Can we assign an exclusive undercover agent department for the Department of Justice? Can we meet all the expenses? Is it possible to handle the additional expenses that may arise? Is it worth making a team?

While they analysed the various aspects of setting up a dedicated secret agency department, the existing Secret Service agency encountered a problem and the media made a mountain out of a molehill.

This is what happened. An officer in the US Navy went missing. A Secret Service agent was assigned the task of finding him. Since the agency had years of experience in this arena, they were able to find him effortlessly. However, the officer wasn't alone. He was with his girlfriend. What was worse was that she wasn't his legitimate girlfriend. He was with a married woman. To put it plain, he was dating and had eloped with another man's wife.

When Secret Service agents discovered this and brought it into the open, the woman's husband became furious. He applied for divorce in a court of law. It was not a problem then. The real problem brewed in the court during the case hearings. When the court asked for the reason for divorce, the man declared, "My wife was in an extramarital relationship with another man. The government Secret Service agency is the witness."

The public became extremely annoyed on hearing this. Looking at extramarital affairs? Is this what the government agencies signed up for? Why do these agencies intrude on the personal lives of the people?

The public became extremely annoyed on hearing this. *Looking at extramarital affairs? Is this what the government agencies signed up for? Why do these agencies intrude on the personal lives of the people?*

The opposition party waiting for such an incident exaggerated everything. A lot of people started to mock the government stating that they were called Secret Service to find out these extramarital and secret relationships.

The government immediately passed an ordinance. "No one should hire the services of Secret Service agents for random jobs."

Upon the release of this ordinance, the Department of Justice / Office of the Attorney General felt extremely happy and relieved. “Hereafter, the government doesn’t have a say. We cannot use the agents from the Department of Treasury. We are free to set up our own undercover services.”

On 26th July 1908, the Federal Bureau of Investigation was born. It was the day an official announcement was made towards setting up the new intelligence department under the control of the Department of Justice. However, the team did not have a distinct name. The agents had to report to Stanley Finch, Chief Examiner of the Department of Justice.

How did the Department of Justice suddenly hire the secret agents (or the examiners)?

It is somewhat hilarious. Already, the examiners who were part of the Secret Service agency had gained experience in working as private detectives. They were novices but very active and always had their focus on doing something innovative. The intelligence bureau of the Department of Justice identified, grabbed them, and hired them as the first set of examiners with the FBI. Not many could spend time in leisure. Tedious tasks awaited their arrival from the day of joining. Needless to say, the Department of Justice was loaded with pending cases.

By the end of the year 1908 ,Charles Bonaparte submitted his annual report to the government He gave a report on the satisfactory performance of the new intelligence team.

Next year, Theodore Roosevelt’s term of presidency came to an end. Following this, Charles Bonaparte also resigned from his Attorney General position. ‘George Wickersham’ was appointed as the new Attorney General. However, he did not contribute to the progression and growth of the FBI. Bonaparte's successor named the force, 'Bureau of Investigation'. For the next few years, the examiners' team was called BOI. A lot of new agents joined the team. Proper training, rules, and regulations were formed. The importance of the investigation bureau increased every year.

Bonaparte's successor named the force, 'Bureau of Investigation'. For the next few years, the examiners' team was called BOI. A lot of new agents joined the team. Proper training, rules, and regulations were formed. The importance of the investigation bureau increased every year.

The major reason behind this growing necessity was that the country was loaded with crimes and cases. The criminals were smart enough to escape from the hands of the law. BOI team was in full force to investigate and arrest the criminals.

In the year 1910, a new act named 'White-Slave Traffic Act' was enforced by the government in the US. However, from the public to the government officials and police force, they called it the 'Mann Act' which was passed by the person named James Robert Mann.

The basic objective of this ordinance was the prohibition of selling white people as slaves. However, on the grounds of reality, the law was harnessed to stop, prevent and control sex trafficking of young women and girls.

During that specific period, the sex industry was booming in the US. It was very active and noticeable. In each place, specific localities or residences called 'red-light areas' were active in this business. While it is not known whether the common people were aware of this, it came to the ears of those who were seeking it. On a simple note, those in need knew about it and made use of it.

The Mann Act did not make any difference in another type of illegal and fraudulent activity. Did it affect counterfeiters, landlords abducting the lands by fraud, and small-time crimes or illegal activities? It did not. To manage and control the various illegal activities and crimes, the number of examiners in the BOI was doubled.

Women who were voluntarily involved in offering sexual favours in the American brothels form a totally different context. Many women were forced and trapped into sex trafficking. The Mann Law helped to punish the criminals who were behind the sex trafficking.

Soon after the ordinance of the Mann Law, the workload of the examiners in the Department of Justice multiplied. It involved scrutinising the ‘red-light areas’, checking on the women in the centres, conducting a complete investigation upon the arrival of a new sex worker to rule out sex trafficking or abduction, taking necessary legal action on people involved in illegal activities, and more.

Some cities do not have any specific red-light areas. However, the business runs hidden from the government. The examiners were accountable to investigate the secret sexual business and make sure no sex trafficking was involved.

The Mann Act did not make any difference in another type of illegal and fraudulent activity. Did it affect counterfeiters, landlords abducting the lands by fraud, and small-time crimes or illegal activities? It did not. To manage and control the various illegal activities and crimes, the number of examiners in the BOI was doubled.

During this period, in addition to the field examiners, the number of people who contributed to an investigation from the back-end called 'support staff' also doubled. The sudden rise in the number of agents also led to an exponential increase in cost. How would they manage? However, the US ignored the fact. The major reason is the First World War.

During the commencement of the First World War in the European countries, BOI had almost 300 field examiners and equally supported by a similar number of employees from the office of the BOI.

The intelligence department formed with 34 examiners in the year 1908 experienced twenty percent growth in the next five or six years. They were allocated an exclusive budget and special authority. The increasing crime rate in the country was the major reason. There was no foreseeable reduction in the criminal population despite enforcing stringent and rigid laws. Due to the increasing usage of automobiles, it had become easier to commit a crime and escape to another place. Local police could not find or restrain criminals.

Since crimes cannot be controlled by the provincial authorities within their boundaries, the importance of National Security continued to increase. There was a constant surge in the numbers, nature, and impact of the cases issued to the BOI examiners. The BOI offices were opened throughout the country.

When the First World War began, Department of Justice examiners were charged with additional responsibilities. They had to be on guard against the foreign personnel invading the country; exercise caution and scrutiny over their local spies and save the crucial information of the country. In fact, the US was a not direct participant in the First World War. The US was just a long-distance spectator of the war in Europe.

When the First World War began, Department of Justice examiners were charged with additional responsibilities. They had to be on guard against the foreign personnel invading the country; exercise caution and scrutiny over their local spies and save the crucial information of the country.

However, Germany's thought process was different. They concluded that America was not just a spectator but supported the Britishers. Germany decided to attack America. Eventually, the US ships were attacked and destroyed at many places by German submarines. It doesn't end there. Germany carried out a bombing attack on US soil.

In the US, the government gradually started losing patience. A breaking point arrived and the country decided to be a direct participant in the war. At a rapid speed, they gathered their forces. Accordingly, the government made an announcement that all youngsters and middle-aged people with good physical health must enrol in military service. Many agreed ,Only a few avoided and ran away citing false reasons.

As the war approached, many people avoided joining the military service. They cited lame reasons to enlist despite having good health. It was a tedious task finding the right people to train in the army.

Mere military force and power of weapons were not sufficient for the US to take part in the world war. They had to be informed about the actions and plans of the rival country in advance. At the same time, they had to ensure that the information about them didn't seep out.

All these important tasks were assigned to the 'Bureau'. They were informed to find the people who ran away avoiding the army. "Ensure that our boundaries remain intact and keep the intruders from the rival countries away."

The Bureau meticulously executed this task. During the First World War, their jurisdiction was increased. Besides, it also resulted in an enhancement in their precision. What would be the result if the government agency gained additional authority and precision? The abundance in confidence led towards ignorance.

The Bureau made a mistake. The incident post the First World War is the worst-case scenario in the history of the FBI.

❑

4
For Oil...

It was months after the 'Palmer Raids'. In the peaceful country, there was a new danger. Anna Brown was the victim. She was twenty five years old. She was of the Osage tribe in the Oklahoma Province, US. She was friendly to everyone ,had no rivals..

One day, she suddenly went missing. All her friends searched for her. But she was no trace . However by the end of May, corpse of Anna found in a decomposed stag

The Osage tribe was shocked. Who caused the death of this poor girl? Is there a ny disease to her? Or did she fall and die?

No, that was not the case. She had a gunshot wound at the back of her head. She was shot at close range. No one had a clue , who had done it or why?

At the same time, another dead body was found who was identified as Charles Whitehorn. He also belonged to the Osage tribe. He was also killed in the same way as Anna.

The local police conducted an inquiry to trace the murderer of both Anna and Charles.But they could not even get the smallest clue. They closed the case with a big question mark! After two months,on July 1921,) Anna's mother, Lizzie Q Kyle also died suspiciously. The police suspected that she was poisoned to death. However, they did not get sufficient evidence, also could not find any clues that linked these three murders.

In February 1923, there was another brutal death. Anna Brown's relative, Henry Roan Horse was shot to death in his car. Four murders on the row and three belonged to the same family. The Osage tribe firmly believed there could be some conspiracy behind it.

Fortunately, for the next one and a half years, there was no specific unpleasant incident that happened to the Osage tribe. The local people and the policemen gradually began to forget the murders.

In February 1923, there was another brutal death. Anna Brown's relative, Henry Roan Horse was shot to death in his car. Four murders on the row and three belonged to the same family. The Osage tribe firmly believed there could be some conspiracy behind it. However, even this time, the police did not get any significant evidence. When they were brainstorming about the suspected people, the next bomb was just dropped.

This time, it was not a bullet shot, but literally an explosive.

Many incidents happened to raise the doubts of the agents. Some purposely delayed the investigation by the detectives. Some confused them by giving different inputs. When requested for an explanation, they said, "Sorry, I don't know anything."

The bomb was thrown on the residence of Anna Brown's sister, Rita Smith. Rita, her husband, and their servant died. The entire residence was destroyed in this blast.

Due to this ,the Osage tribe lost trust in the police . They directly contacted the government and gave a petition requesting, "We are being attacked and someone is murdered every month. Yet, the local policemen failed to find even a trace of the murderers. You must investigate and help us find the people involved."

The Bureau of Investigation, which was incorporated fifteen years ago, handled the cases related to the Department of Justice. They did not investigate the individual murder cases. Yet, this was totally different. Tribes were affected by these circumstances, and it required the intervention of the federal government. Eventually, the government assigned the case to the Bureau and wanted them to investigate the chain of murders.

In fact, before the intervention of the Bureau, many police officers and private detectives tried their chance. However, they could find nothing.

What did it indicate? Either, the murders were random. Or, this might have been a well-planned act by some big shots in the country. Many incidents happened to raise the doubts of the agents. Some purposely delayed the investigation by the detectives. Some confused them by giving different inputs. When requested for an explanation, they said, "Sorry, I don't know anything."

The Bureau's special agents too faced the same problems. Despite their strenuous efforts, they could not find any clue. During the investigation the Osage people did not utter even a single word. The detectives did not know how to proceed.

Hence, the Bureau experts locked themselves in a room. They believed that all these murders happened for a single reason. On this basis, they assessed a lot of factors. Based on their assessments, they suspected one person, Molly Gayle.

Who was Molly Gayle?

Molly Gayle was the sister of the two dead women, Anna Brown who was shot dead and Rita Smith who died in a bomb blast at her residence. She was the daughter of Lizzi, who was poisoned to death.Now the question arises , what did she gain by killing her own mother and sisters? It was nothing small. She gained more than half a million dollars, every year.

Anna, Rita, and Lizzi belonged to the Osage tribe. Were they even rich?

Osage tribes migrated to different parts of the country and lived in different places. They lived in districts like Missouri, Kansas and Arkansas. However, a considerable population lived in Oklahoma. In the year 1897, an important turning-point happened in the lives of the Osage tribe. At Oklahoma, (the place they own) an abundance of oil resources was discovered.

According to the Federal Law, when an oil resource or any other resource is extracted from a specific place, a percentage from the profit on sales must be provided to the owners of the place. This is called royalty.

It is common that oil prices spike every year and the demand increases proportionately. Due to the oil resources in Oklahoma, everyone believed that the Osage tribe would receive billions of dollars as royalty every year.

It is common that oil prices spike every year and the demand increases proportionately. Due to the oil resources in Oklahoma, everyone believed that the Osage tribe would receive billions of dollars as royalty every year.

At that time, the total population of the Osage tribe was less than a few thousand. The royalty paid by the government was distributed equally. Not just once or twice, but once every year. They get paid every year, after their lifetime. The royalty would be paid to their heirs and family. It is like the goose yielding golden eggs. Like winning a lottery, the Oklahoma Osage tribe had heaps of money.

Let's now come back to the chain of murders. The murdered Anna, Rita, and their mother Lizzi were receiving their share of royalty. Who get benefits when they are dead? Who will receive their share of royalty?

Lizzi had three daughters, Molly Gayle was the only one alive. She would be the successor to her family's fortune. When all the others were dead in her family , she would be the only who would receive a hefty sum as royalty. Hence, the Bureau decided that Molly might have hired people to kill her family.

Yet, there were no traces of evidence. Then they deepened their investigation,and explored the personal life of Molly and found an important clue.

Ernest Burkhart, Molly's husband was one of those relatives of William Hale. Ernest was innocent. He used to nod in favour of whatever William said. This shifted the focus from Ernest to William. The Bureau suspected that William and his team could lead them to the deaths of Anna and her family.

Molly's husband was Ernest Burkhart. Ernest's relative, William Hale was one of the richest men in the neighbourhood. None of the Oklahoma residents call William Hale by name. The tribes addressed him as 'King of Osage Mountains'. Of course, he named himself that.

In fact, Oklahoma was not William Hale birthplace. He did not grow up there too. He was from Texas in search of a job. He wanted to earn big money either by hook or crook. Later, he called a few close relatives and settled there. He also developed a big group of followers who nodded to whatever he said.

William Hale was a big-time influencer and the tribe had great respect towards him. Due to his affluence, the government officials and policemen could not reach him.

Ernest Burkhart, Molly's husband was one of those relatives of William Hale. Ernest was innocent. He used to nod in favour of whatever William said. This shifted the focus from Ernest to William. The Bureau suspected that William and his team could lead them to the deaths of Anna and her family. The investigation continued.

When the Osage tribe came to know about it, they tried to hide from the Bureau. They displayed fear while talking to the detectives. Unfortunately, some people came forward and shared some clues only to misguide the Bureau. They spent their time and money in vain.

In the following weeks, the Bureau tried in every way possible but couldn't find anything. They understood that no one would say anything against their king. They decided to attack them indirectly.

The detectives disguised themselves in four different ways. One man disguised as an insurance agent and associated with the Osage tribe. Another person became a cattle vendor. The third one became an oil dealer and the fourth detective disguised himself as a physician. Hence, from the beginning, the local people never suspected them. All the four detectives developed new friendships, business relations, and gained the Osage tribe's trust.

Later, they started an investigation. It was done casually like friendly talk and gossip. Now, the Osage people had conversations with them. They effortlessly revealed many things. The Bureau clearly followed it and finally found solid evidence. One of the close relatives of William spoke the truth for the first time to the Bureau . Also he was an important part in William's group. He played an important part in the murders.

Now the Bureau finally found the accurate reasons behind the murders and how they plotted the murders. The collection of the remaining pieces of evidence was not difficult. It was the biggest success for the team and they reaped a big success despite being in disguise for months. Without any benefit of doubt, they arrested William with solid evidence. The Osage tribe was shocked and couldn't believe what they heard.

Everyone was aware William Hale was a rogue. However, no one expected that he might go to the extent of murdering a whole family. Here was the truth. William Hale had meticulously planned for the murder. He had the chance to earn half a million dollars every year. When he moved to Oklahoma, he became hungry for money. He spent days and nights thinking about how to attract the oil resource royalty towards him.

Everyone was aware William Hale was a rogue. However, no one expected that he might go to the extent of murdering a whole family. Here was the truth. William Hale had meticulously planned for the murder. He had the chance to earn half a million dollars every year.

But there was a major problem. He was not from the Osage tribe. No one would volunteer to offer their oil royalty to him. So, he decided to include someone from his family in the Osage tribe. He picked Ernest and married him to Molly. Now Molly had one share of royalty from oil resources. When she was killed, her husband would get the royalty. Since Ernest was just a puppet, William would enjoy the royalty.

This wasn't sufficient for William Hale.So , he decided not to kill Molly. Instead, he murdered her mother, sisters, and some relatives.

We are aware of these four or five murders only. At the same time, he murdered many other people from the tribes for the royalty from oil resources and insurance money and those who were willing to testify against him at the court. He must have killed more than two dozen tribal people.

Due to these murders, Molly started receiving a lot of royalty funds. Hale decided to kill her too. He was planning to poison Molly when the Bureau encircled him. Had they delayed, she would have been dead too.

At the same time, the number of cases filed against William was increasing. Money played at all the places. Some people changed sides and all the crucial evidence was destroyed. Many worried that they might get caught.

Thankfully, when William plotted to kill Molly, she had moved to a different place. Her life was saved.

At the same time, the number of cases filed against William was increasing. Money played at all the places. Some people changed sides and all the crucial evidence was destroyed. Many worried that they might get caught.

Even during this uptight situation, Osage tribes were calm and handled the situation diligently. They wanted the criminals to be punished. So, they collected money among themselves for the case. They also made sure that no one changed their side for money. The Bureau also had additional concerns on this case.

To prove the guilty of all the crimes without any benefit of doubt, the Bureau conducted the case meticulously. They prepared the report that was made into several thousand pages. We would wonder at the comprehensive report which is available for free to the public's view.

The crimes of William Hale were proven in the court of law..Finally William Hale received a life sentence after eight years of Anna's death. Many of his gang members were also sentenced to several years of imprisonment.

During the case hearings, the crime rate in the country gradually increased. Gangsters took many cities under their control. No one felt secure and protected.

However, the Bureau were not able to investigate directly. According to the Federal Law, handling the crimes was not in their league. They could only investigate the crimes that are tagged as a federal violation. Besides, many gangsters ruled with dangerous weapons. They would destroy the detectives in a few seconds if they appeared before the gangsters, unarmed.

What was the role of the Bureau now? Were they going to stay put as mere onlookers? Or would they look for other means to control them like how they handled William Hale?

❑

5
Action and Intelligence

It was the beginning of October 1925. It had been one and a half years since Edgar Hoover took charge as the director of the Bureau. In this short duration, he made lots of changes that earned him honour and respect among the ruling party.

But there was a problem, all the changes that he incorporated were at the administrative level. It was undeniable that these amendments enhanced the efficiency of the management. However, there were no differences in the duties between then and now.

An office may have different types of duties. Imagine, you do just one or two tasks effectively. You get a manager or supervisor who teaches you to carry out two more additional tasks. They guide you and make you perform well. Hoover implemented these types of changes in the Bureau.

Yet, at the same time, the office has other duties pending execution. It is more important than what you do now. However, you do not have sufficient skills, qualifications or equipment right at the moment. Still, you think somehow you can learn and move ahead.

There was a twenty five year-old young man named Martin James Turkin from Chicago. He became involved in crime at a very tender age. His full-time business was the sale of cars stolen by him.

Edgar Hoover planned similarly. He decided that the Bureau would control and eradicate the gangsters and handle National Security. He also persistently looked for ways that could help him.

There was a twenty five year-old young man named Martin James Turkin from Chicago. He became involved in crime at a very tender age. His full-time business was the sale of cars stolen by him.

Martin was an intelligent guy. He would not sell the car which he stole in the same district. In oder to sell those car he cross the boundaries and sell them in different provinces. Due to this, the police from both provinces struggled extremely to trace him and take legal action on him.

Apart from legal action, should he not be caught? All the time, he would zoom around in the stolen cars. How could someone catch or even trace him? This case was assigned to the Bureau.

Martin stole a car on 11th October 1925, in Chicago. Soon after receiving this information, an agent chased him. Martin remained cool. He suddenly picked up his gun and shot the agent. When this news spread, the Bureau could not believe it. Civilians were taken aback by this incident.

The reason behind the shocking experience from the public was that Bureau agent Edwin Shanahan did not fight back when Martin shot him. "Should he have not shot him at least below the knees?" The civilians who were experts from reading crime novels felt sorry for the dead agent.

How could Edwin shoot? He didn't have a gun.

This was an even bigger shock to the public. What, Bureau agents do not have guns? Why?

The responsibility of the Bureau is to investigate and arrest the robbers, burglars, and those who are involved in illegal activities. Shouldn't they have at least a gun for their safety?

"Yes, it is essential," said Edgar Hoover. "We are helpless. We are not permitted to use guns."

"So, let's amend the law."

"Yes, we can. However, we have to find Martin. We must take him down. Otherwise, Edwin Shanahan's soul won't rest in peace." Edgar Hoover uttered the sentimental movie dialogue and left the place.

The Bureau was not aggressive in chasing the criminals till that incident. They were determined to seek justice for the murder of Edwin and arrest Martin. Eventually, Hoover had gotten involved in this task of finding Martin.

However, as Martin was a smart criminal, they couldn't trace him easily. They had to travel across at least half the country to arrest him after two years. In January 1926, he was arrested. After thorough hearings at the court, he was sentenced to thirty five years in jail.

The dedication and intensity of Hoover and the Bureau in this case was not just focused on justifying the murder of Edwin. If Martin escaped, all criminals would start threatening or even shooting the Bureau agents.

The dedication and intensity of Hoover and the Bureau in this case was not just focused on justifying the murder of Edwin. If Martin escaped, all criminals would start threatening or even shooting the Bureau agents.

After the murder of Edwin Shanahan, the crime rate increased in the next several months. Local police investigated most of the cases. The Bureau could not interfere directly.

In 1929, another agent Paul Reynolds was murdered. Edgar Hoover demanded using guns for self-protection. However, no one responded.

The federal government did not ignore their demand. When compared with the US police, Bureau agents would not carry guns throughout the day. Most of the investigation would be among the public. Rarely, the agents were at risk. During those circumstances, they could get protection from the police. The government decided they did not need guns.

Edgar Hoover refuted it. If the agents had guns, they could easily plan for bolder activities. However, they waited for the opportune time. They decided to keep it aside for some time and as they feared, another terrible incident happened.

Frank Nash did not want to spend a major part of his life in jail. In the year 1930, Frank Nash escaped from the Leavenworth jail. The Bureau was assigned the task of tracing him. In the next few months, various agents from the Bureau hunted for Frank Nash throughout the country.

The man behind the incident was Frank 'Jelly' Nash. He was the most wanted criminal, famed for bank robbery. Police and Bureau agents tried to hunt him in many cases. He would get arrested, go to jail, and after release, commit more crimes.

More or less, he had become a regular visitor to the jail. However, he got stuck in a major crime in 1924. He was sentenced to a twenty five years jail term. He was locked in the Leavenworth jail in Kansas.

Frank Nash did not want to spend a major part of his life in jail. In the year 1930, Frank Nash escaped from the Leavenworth jail. The Bureau was assigned the task of tracing him. In the next few months, various agents from the Bureau hunted for Frank Nash throughout the country. No one was aware of his whereabouts or who helped him.

After a long search, ion 15th June, 1933,Frank Nash was caught. He was arrested in Arkansas and sent to Kansas jail.

The news about Frank Nash being caught and subsequently locked up at Kansas made his partners anxious. They were determined to save him and executed a plan. On June 17, the vehicle that carried Frank Nash and the police officers who arrested him along with the Bureau agents entered the Kansas Railway station around 7:15 a.m. Everyone stepped down. They brought Frank Nash with utmost security and transferred him into a car. The next minute, suddenly some people appeared and started firing guns.

The death of Ray Caffrey created a sensation in the public. Many questioned why the Bureau was not permitted to use and not issued weapons even after the change in the ruling party. Edgar Hoover also made a strong demand to his senior authorities.

All happened in a few seconds. The air was cloudy with smoke and there was a lot of blood. No one was able to get a clear picture of what had happened. Before the policemen attempted to attack, they were gone. The worst thing was not the death of Frank Nash. While this attack was planned to save him, three police officers and a Bureau agent were also dead.

This incident is known as 'Kansas City Massacre'. It is very important in the history of the FBI. In this attack, after the death of an agent named Ray Caffrey, the most anticipated weapon power was allocated to the Bureau.

The death of Ray Caffrey created a sensation in the public. Many questioned why the Bureau was not permitted to use and not issued weapons even after the change in the ruling party. Edgar Hoover also made a strong demand to his senior authorities.

At last, on their demands , the government allowed agents to use automatic rifles for their protection. That was just the beginning. Later, gradually, the Bureau was permitted to use different types of guns. The new agents underwent mandatory training in using weapons.

As expected by Edgar Hoover, many agents showed greater interest and dedication in their work than ever. All the small-time criminals were brought under control. The Bureau had some big whales on their list.

Edgar Hoover proposed an idea. He wanted an exclusive Technology Research Department.

Now we are well informed about the importance of science and technology in crime investigation. From the crime scene, analysing the fingerprints to DNA study, this department had so many advancements. Yet, at the beginning of the 20s, when Edgar Hoover proposed this idea, no one took him seriously. "Sir, are you drunk today? Please think about what you are saying. Go home safely."

Edgar Hoover did not lose his faith. He persistently demanded the setting up of an exclusive technology research centre. He did not stay until getting the approval and budget allocated.

Meanwhile, Hoover with his fellow officers discussed the importance of technology. "The task for which you take days to complete or analyse can be done in less than a minute. It is good for us to learn it."

Edgar Hoover's motivation helped many Bureau agents to learn about science, the latest technology, and inventions. They also brainstormed whether they could use it in their daily jobs. Still, the technology research centre was not set up. They sought assistance from external experts as and when needed.

Since the crime rate in the country was increasing at the beginning of the 30s, Bureau agents also turned more active in their investigations. Of course, they also needed a lot of technical support.

At the Bureau, Special Agent Charles Appel approached Hoover. He said, "Chicago is organizing a training programme on how to scientifically investigate crimes. I would like to participate."

At the Bureau, Special Agent Charles Appel approached Hoover. He said, "Chicago is organizing a training programme on how to scientifically investigate crimes. I would like to participate."

"Please, go ahead," agreed Hoover. The Bureau paid for the travel and all other expenses,

In 1931, during April and May, Charles learnt a lot of technological practices in the training. Analysing the signature, handwriting and letters, determining what type of typewriter is used for typing letters, information about various weapons, and scientific knowledge required for investigation were few of the many things he learnt. He travelled back with a lot of new plans for the Bureau. Unfortunately, nothing was implemented immediately because ofbudget problem.

Edgar Hoover motivated Charles persistently. "The government will permit us to start a technology lab anyway. So, you must be ready to manage it."

Charles spent a lot of time analysing how to invest his learnings in the best interests of the Bureau. He expanded his friends circle by having discussions with the technology experts who visited the Bureau and offered help. He also constantly came up with new ideas.

In the middle of 1932, Charles Appel created a detailed report about the technology research centre of the Bureau. It included where to start, when to start, how to manage, expenses, how to earn a return on investment, and many more details. As usual, Edgar Hoover welcomed all ideas.

> *Edgar Hoover's long-time dream came true. Hereafter, Bureau agents need not rely on papers and other evidence. It was possible to decide everything based on scientific research. Even the most difficult job was done easily. It also made it easy to handle a large number of cases and solve the trickier cases.*

"Technology research centre helps identify the crimes in advance or resolve them quickly. The police department and other federal departments may also use our research centre for technological investigations."

This time, the government agreed to the ideas of Charles and Hoover. They started hunting for the place and equipment for the Bureau tech lab.

According to the records, 24th November 1932 was the official launch of the FBI Technology Centre. However, it started functioning a few days before. With a microscope, an ultraviolet machine, a tool that assessed the internal part of the gun, and more equipment, Charles started his work.

Edgar Hoover's long-time dream came true. Hereafter, Bureau agents need not rely on papers and other evidence. It was possible to decide everything based on scientific research. Even the most difficult job was done easily. It also made it easy to handle a large number of cases and solve the trickier cases.

> *Charles was ready to give the ransom. There were more ransom notes with demands for more money. A doctor agreed to be the 'go-between'. He met a man named 'John', gave seventy thousand dollars as ransom, and left.*

Bureau agents distributed handouts to everyone asking them to use the services of their tech lab. Charles Appel was eagerly waiting for someone to assign the first task.

Initially, the tasks that needed Charles's expertise were very simple. Despite that, he executed them with great enthusiasm. However, the Bureau did not get a chance to justify the necessity of a tech lab. Until they received the 'Lindbergh Kidnap Case'.

Charles Lindbergh was a renowned US pilot. He created a record handling a flight across the Atlantic Pacific as a single pilot. He got married to Annie in the year 1929. They had a baby boy next year. He was named Charles Jnr. Post his Atlantic record, Charles received a lot of media exposure. To avoid the media limelight, he purchased a big farmhouse in New Jersey and settled there. Despite this, the paparazzi chased him. On 1st March 1932, his son was kidnapped.

Charles was shocked. Who had kidnapped a one and a half-yearold child?

Immediately he got the answer. They got the letter stating: "If you don't give us fifty thousand dollars, we will kill your baby."

Charles was ready to give the ransom. There were more ransom notes with demands for more money. A doctor agreed to be the 'go-between'. He met a man named 'John', gave seventy thousand dollars as ransom , and left.

What about the child? There was still no information on that. The police offered a reward for any information related to the kidnapping and tried to trace the currency bills given as ransom. Unfortunately, they were only able to find the dead body of the baby.

Who was John, who collected the ransom and killed the baby? New Jersey police struggled a lot without any proper evidence.

Almost at the same time, the technology research centre of the Bureau of Investigation was set up in Washington. The police enquired if they could help in the Lindberg case. Charles Appel investigated the type of letters they received—whether they were typed out or handwritten.

"Do all letters have similar handwriting or were there any changes?"

"It was all similar."

"Do you suspect anyone?"

"We have random suspicions on around three hundred people."

"Bring the handwriting samples of all those three hundred suspects along with the letters written by the kidnappers. We will verify everything in the lab and come to a conclusion."

"What if the kidnapper modified the handwriting?"

"Regardless of efforts made by a person to change the handwriting, a small line or a character would show up the original writing style. Just give us the samples. We will take care of the rest."

> *Charles Appel's confidence stunned the police. They provided everything he asked for. At the same time, the police also scrutinised whether the ransom amount taken from Lindbergh was spent by the kidnappers.*

Charles Appel's confidence stunned the police. They provided everything he asked for. At the same time, the police also scrutinised whether the ransom amount taken from Lindbergh was spent by the kidnappers. Based on tracing currency note numbers, the police planned to find the locality and arrest him.

Meanwhile, Charles Appel analysed all the letters he received. He could not decide based on the letters. However, he was sure that the letters must have been written by a German. Even the police concluded on the same. On 19th September 1934, they arrested a German as a suspect, named Bruno Richard Hauptmann.

Immediately, Charles Appel verified the signature of Hauptmann. Without any doubt, he concluded, both are the same.

"Will you say the same in the court?"

"Sure."

Based on the witness provided by Charles Appel, Hauptmann was proven guilty. He was issued a death sentence. After the sensational case of Lindbergh's kidnap, the Bureau's technology research centre gained popularity. Policemen sought help from Charles Appel in many cases.

More importantly, witnesses would be changed by offering money or threatening in the cases that involved gangsters. They could do nothing with the scientifically proven evidence. Eventually, the Bureau's support helped to a great extent to control and reduce the gangster games.

In the beginning, the Bureau of Investigation Technical Lab functioned as a one-man-show, but upon persistent effort from Charles Appel, it gained popularity and growth. Additional employees, equipment, new technology, exclusive building, and more development were evident.

At the same time, almost all agents used the support of the technology lab. The importance of the lab increased for both Bureau agents and external departments. Another major transformation happened at the same time. On 1st July 1935, the Bureau of Investigation provided a suffix, 'Federal'.

What is Federal?

It is similar to what we called 'Central Government' in our country.

The only difference is, in the US, the states have more power (The name US says it all). So, it doesn't mean a power higher than the power of the states but a power that combines the rule of all states. It is called federal government. The American governing body of Congress is a part of this government.

The Bureau of Investigation functioned as a part of this federal government. To mention it, the name was changed to 'Federal Bureau of Investigation' (FBI).

❑

6
Double Trouble

In the middle of the 30s, the US faced two more problems; one from communists and another from fascists.

When the Bolshevik government commenced during 1917, under the leadership of Lenin, the US became wary of communism. The country looked at everyone suspiciously as communists during any riot. The American president was distressed whenever he heard any industry calling a strike. He suspected that Russian spies were trying to instigate strikes.

In the next few years, the population of communists continued to increase. Who are associated with communists? What are they planning to do in our country? Are they stealing our secrets? Or trying to implement their policies? The federal government did not have a clear picture.

Fifteen years had gone by since the start of the Russian communist revolution. Hitler had the upper hand in Germany. When people heard his speech, everyone concluded that his desire to evolve would not end with Germany.

In the year 1934, US President 'Franklin D Roosevelt' called the FBI. He wanted to make a list of Germans living in the country. Most importantly, he wanted the list of Germans who had connections with international spies.

At the same time, a lot of Germans lived in the US. How many supported Hitler's Nazi party? What type of threat could they pose to the country? Another trouble started.

In the year 1934, US President 'Franklin D Roosevelt' called the FBI. He wanted to make a list of Germans living in the country. Most importantly, he wanted the list of Germans who had connections with international spies. Also he wanted to find out the US citizens who spied for Germany.

Hearing this, the Bureau looked worried. Beyond small-time criminals, local criminals and gang leaders, the Bureau had also started investigating international crimes.

The FBI head, Edgar Hoover once worked as a librarian. He was an expert in organising books. He carried his organising skill to the Bureau. Especially, he excelled in the fingerprint collection section, aligning and sectioning the crime details. With all his efforts, the FBI technological lab functioned effectively.

Then, the FBI started to find and weed out the people and foreigners trying to threaten or threatening the country. *Who were the Germans who migrated to the US? Which were the German families that were born and lived here? What about their political interests? Who were friends with them? What were the activities they were involved in? The places they work? Were they found doing any suspicious activity? What are the secrets they might come to know? Would it harm the country?* Every aspect was carefully analysed.

Based on the information, a list of Germans was prepared that were likely to cause damage to the country. No immediate action was taken. However, everyone was closely monitored.

Importantly, while the FBI was making a list of suspicious Germans and Russians, the Second World War happened. It was unknown whether the US would take part in the Second World War.

Eventually, all the information collected by the Bureau was secured only for internal purposes. Only in some specific circumstances, foreign spies or detectives would do something big and get caught. During those incidents, the FBI and policemen intervened directly and arrested them. Otherwise, people who were not troublesome were left alone. The federal government just put them aside, considering they could handle it when something bad happened.

In the year 1939.,the Second World War began. Hitler's army forcefully attacked and captured most of Europe at a rapid pace. Mussolini and Italy joined hands with him. Japan became their long-distance ally.

The US awakened. They put aside their scrutiny of communists. The FBI was ready with a comprehensive list of Germans, Italians and Japanese living in the country. They did not take any action and stayed put. They ignored the attacks on Asia. The country did not want to interfere as long as Hitler, Mussolini and the Japanese did not disturb them.

In the year 1939.,the Second World War began. Hitler's army forcefully attacked and captured most of Europe at a rapid pace. Mussolini and Italy joined hands with him. Japan became their long-distance ally.

However, the US was not able to stay away for a longer time. They immediately entered the war when Japan bombed Pearl harbour. In the end, they demolished Japan by blasting the country with two bombs.

When the country started the battle in the Second World War, the FBI started its full wing. As per the list of 'foreigners' they created, they arrested everyone whom they suspected. It led to an arrest of three thousand people in three days. Within a few days, President 'Roosevelt' assigned a new task to the Bureau. "Working on internal affairs is not enough. You have to look out for the external dangers too."

There is no necessity that haters of the country must intrude and conduct a riot. They can effortlessly ruin the peace sitting from anywhere. They could collect secret information and send it to their management. To prohibit this, Bureau started another wing called 'Special Intelligence Service'. The agents who joined this wing started investigating and watching over other countries that shared borders with America.

The FBI took care of the internal affairs for the past thirty years. So, they did not have enough experience or exposure to go beyond their boundaries and investigate external affairs. Involving in the secret activities outside the country, collection of data, taking photographs, classifying and copying the documents, sending them to the country, getting money, etc. involved a high degree of risk. They needed a lot of training to work tactfully without getting caught or escape when they get caught.

Bureau agents just embraced these challenges. They understood the political facets, culture, and prevailing practices of various countries and assigned special detectives in the respective places. They developed trust with the Americans and local people who lived there by offering money and other favours. Eventually, they tried to collect and send the details of undercover operations of Germany and its friendly alliances to the US.

From 1940 to the next six years, the information provided by the Special Intelligence Service wing helped in the identification of hundreds of intruders, war criminals and spies. Their radio devices were confiscated.

From 1940 to the next six years, the information provided by the Special Intelligence Service wing helped in the identification of hundreds of intruders, war criminals and spies. Their radio devices were confiscated.

In some circumstances, the FBI went ahead. The FBI used the radio confiscated from the intruders and sent fake messages to confuse the rival countries. Many times, the Nazi force believed these messages and got trapped.

The Bureau just indicated a starting point and the civilians explored the way. From the next day, the FBI received constant calls about suspects, complaints, brave speeches, fearful talks, requests, and more. The FBI did not ignore even a single call.

Due to this, at one point, Nazi leaders suspected the news and information received from their own (original) agents. Across the world, Germans created a chain of spy wings. This confusion reduced the impact and eventually led to failure.

At the same time, the FBI also ensured to prevent the Germans or its allies from invading America. The suspected people in the list of the FBI had been constantly monitored. Even if they moved an inch in the wrong direction, they were immediately arrested.

Besides, the FBI made a request to the civilians in the US. "This is the time we must be very careful—like detectives and army men. Be on your guard. If you find anything or anyone suspicious around your neighbourhood, immediately inform us."

The Bureau just indicated a starting point and the civilians explored the way. From the next day, the FBI received constant calls about suspects, complaints, brave speeches, fearful talks, requests, and more. The FBI did not ignore even a single call.

They verified every call, included the list of names in the suspect list to watch or be arrested.

Due to the cautious activities throughout the world, the Second World War, no suspicious dangerous activity was found. The crucial information, army secrets, and other war preparations were secure to the end.

What was Germany doing exactly around this time? Did they just exclude America from their list?

No, it was not the case. In some way or the other, they persistently tried to spy on the US. They prepared many undercover spies in different ways. But every time, whether due to lack of experience or training, they were caught by the traps laid by the FBI. The civilians informed all suspected activities and suspicious people to the Bureau.

On 12th June 1942, a submarine from Germany reached the US (New York Long Island). There were four spies, George Dasch, Ernst Burger, Heinrich Heinck, and Richard Quirin. Post- midnight, they stepped into the city. They removed their army uniforms and wore casual attire. As planned, they started executing their plans.

Yet, there was a problem. The country was not as incapable as they imagined. The US tightened the force around their boundaries across the Bay Area. A policeman who was patrolling around the shores found these four men and their weapons.

They immediately passed the information to the head of the Bureau. They found a lot of weapons, equipment and dresses on their inspection. Eventually, they confirmed the identity of the intruders as Germans. All this information was immediately given to the FBI. The hunt began.

The FBI made the most of this opportunity. Based on the information provided by George Dasch, FBI agents arrested all eight agents sent by Germany. This is just a sample incident. There are many instances where the Bureau captured the undercover agents of Germany and its alliances.

During the same time, four German agents entered via Florida. They quickly went into hiding. The FBI agents also worked secretly in search of those intruders. They decided to capture those Nazi agents without causing any disturbance or damage to the civilians.

Meanwhile, the German agent named George Dasch developed a hatred towards his own country. He might have been frightened by the extreme security of the US. He decided to turn the tables and support the US.

The FBI made the most of this opportunity. Based on the information provided by George Dasch, FBI agents arrested all eight agents sent by Germany.

This is just a sample incident. There are many instances where the Bureau captured the undercover agents of Germany and its alliances. So, after the attack of Pearl harbour, Second World War did not have any negative impact or pose any risk to the US.

During the middle of the 40s, Hitler was defeated, followed by Mussolini. After the drastic incident of Hiroshima and Nagasaki, Japan also surrendered. Finally, the Second World

War ended after taking a lot of lives. Due to this war, the FBI underwent a lot of transformation. Especially, the size of the Bureau. It had 2,400 members in the year 1940. In the next four years, the growth was five times bigger.

At the same time, the growth was planned. Almost all the FBI agents and employees had rigorous training. The efficiency of the Bureau surpassed all the expectations.

The war ended and peace began. *Do we need so many FBI agents? Or should we cut down the numbers?*

Without the need for termination of agents, another war just began. This time, the good old friends of the US turned into their rivals.

❑

7
New Rival

Have you watched Charlie Chaplin's, *Modern Times*? There is an interesting humour scene in it.

Charlie Chaplin is seen walking down the street. A truck drives past him. It has a red flag. When Chaplin is looking at the flag, it falls down. Immediately, Chaplin picks it and calls out to the driver.

Despite of the loud shouts, the driver cannot hear him. He continues to drive. As Chaplin is determined to give him the flag some way or the other. So, holding the flag, he runs, to chase the vehicle.

While Chaplin is running with the flag in his hand, people believe it to be a kind of revolt. Quickly, labourers in large numbers form a procession and follow him. Unknowingly,

Chaplin becomes a leader to a massive procession. It was just an imaginary scene. However, in real life, many big shots also have similar erroneous thoughts and misunderstandings. These types of misconceptions and finding faults transformed the life of Charlie Chaplin upside down.

Characters in Chaplin's movie are mostly poor and underprivileged. They don't even have access to the basic necessities like food, clothing and shelter, and suffered from poverty. Chaplin expressed their daily troubles in comic ways.

Why did Charlie Chaplin suddenly pop up in the story of the FBI?

This is because, Charlie Chaplin was born in England, and followed his career in the US. He entered the film industry and became a renowned celebrity.

From the beginning, Charlie Chaplin's movies discussed specific types of people. Who were the people who repeatedly appeared in his movies? Who was characterised as good and bad? What were the problems they faced? What were the solutions proposed by Chaplin through these characters? When we think from this viewpoint, we can understand better:

Characters in Chaplin's movie are mostly poor and underprivileged. They don't even have access to the basic necessities like food, clothing and shelter, and suffered from poverty. Chaplin expressed their daily troubles in comic ways. The major reason behind the portrayal of poverty in his movies—which he experienced in his younger years. Based on his experiences, he decided to shoot films about underprivileged people.

However, when he talked about the poor, at least for comparison, he had to talk about the rich also. When he displayed the luxury of the rich, he could show the emptiness of the poor. This practical portrayal made people view him as a communist.

Since 1920, each movie of Charlie Chaplin was scrutinized by the senior officials of the FBI. *Did he support the poor? Or did he instigate the poor to go against the rich?* A team persistently scrutinized everything.

In fact, during those years, all his movies focused on humour. However, the government suspected that he might plan for a big revolution through humour. They decided to keep an eye on him.

The FBI's suspicion of Chaplin looked fair from a viewpoint. Films were powerful media that could easily create an impact. It would be an easy task to spread hateful opinions about the government to reach the civilians. It happened in every other country.

The FBI's suspicion of Chaplin looked fair from a viewpoint. Films were powerful media that could easily create an impact. It would be an easy task to spread hateful opinions about the government to reach the civilians. It happened in every other country.

During those days, a celebrity like Charlie Chaplin criticizing the government could lead to a revolution. His fans and public would turn aggressive. Of course, these were the fears of the government.

So, the Bureau watched all his moves and scrutinized every activity. When he acted in a comical scene where an employee kicks the nose of the employer, the Bureau wrote a report that he instigated people to hit their employers on the nose.

Sounds unbelievable, right? That the FBI would go such extremes. However, all this was true. Almost for twenty years, the Bureau scrutinized every movie of Chaplin's. All his close friends and relatives were investigated. A lot of complaints were made about Chaplin.

However, the investigations and interrogations were undisclosed. They could not prove that Charlie Chaplin was guilty of any crime. If the Bureau made allegations on Chaplin just based on assumptions, people would make fun of them. So, the FBI was looking for a good opportunity to attack Chaplin. For almost twenty years. And, their patience was finally rewarded.

In the year 1940, Chaplin's movie, '*The Great Dictator*' was released. It mocked the most horrific ruler, Hitler. Both Hitler and Chaplin had a similar toothbrush and moustache. They even had similar facial features. A friend of Chaplin named Alexander Korda told him to make a comical movie on Hitler.

Chaplin appreciated this and immediately wanted to execute it. He wrote the screenplay and directed it.

There were a horrendous dictator and a poor hairdresser. Both had similar appearances. The story was about their similarity in appearances, how they get interchanged, and the confusions that follow. The movie also delivered a strong message against the war.

This preaching about avoiding war turned out to be a trump

card to the Bureau to take action on Chaplin. As a result, the Bureau started claiming that Chaplin had political ambitions.

In 1942, a woman named Joan Perry filed a case against Chaplin. She stated, "I am pregnant. Charlie Chaplin is the father of my baby."

> *The FBI wanted to investigate the case. Already, Charlie Chaplin had married several young girls of sixteen years of age. Now, he was stuck with another problem. This was only a minor case. Yet, finally the FBI felt it was their time and wanted to take down Chaplin.*

The FBI wanted to investigate the case. Already, Charlie Chaplin had married several young girls of sixteen years of age. Now, he was stuck with another problem. This was only a minor case. Yet, finally the FBI felt it was their time and wanted to take down Chaplin.

There was no connection between Joan Perry's complaint and the Bureau suspecting him to be a communist. They somehow wanted to bring down Chaplin's fame and plant suspicions about him in the minds of civilians. Then, whatever the complaints made against him, people would believe them blindly. This was the secret plan of the government.

So, to increase the importance of the case, a lot of complaints were lodged against Chaplin. They even lodged a case of him abducting and sexually assaulting minor girls. All sections of media blamed him.

There was no DNA test to verify whether Chaplin was the father of the child carried by Joan Perry. So, the Court of Justice ordered a blood test after the birth of a baby girl. The lab results favoured Chaplin. It was medically proven that Chaplin could not be the father of that baby.

However, the court did not agree to the results. They gave a verdict opposing Chaplin and declared that Chaplin must pay for the support of the baby. As the FBI expected, this case caused a red stain on Charlie Chaplin. So, a lot of people directly complained about him.

The first complaint was calling him a communist. What is wrong if Chaplin was a communist? When someone is called a communist in the US, he is a traitor. Besides, he was not an American citizen. He was just living in the country for many years. He worked there. He earned, invested, and had all his properties in the US. Yet, he was a British citizen.

The first complaint was calling him a communist. What is wrong if Chaplin was a communist? When someone is called a communist in the US, he is a traitor. Besides, he was not an American citizen. He was just living in the country for many years. He worked there. He earned, invested, and had all his properties in the US.

This information worked against Chaplin. The magazines started writing ghastly stuff about Chaplin. “He is an immigrant, and is trying to ruin the peace of the country.”

Unfortunately, Chaplin never had a chance to talk in his favour. During the press meet, the journalists planned and pulled his leg. They twisted and modified his answers in print. So, when Chaplin became angry at their cheap tactics, the journalists used that in their favour and cast Chaplin in a negative light.

Chaplin experienced almost ten terrible years. Every day, he woke up to some complaint about him. It looked like everyone was determined to find fault with Chaplin. He favoured Russia, he evaded tax, he was involved in smuggling weapons, he hid four warcraft at his home, and more allegations.

People abused him everywhere. Regardless, no case was legally filed against him. It was very strange. Beyond this, even the FBI were not brave enough to interrogate him in person. They had no evidence. He was not left alone, despite his persistent efforts to convey that he was not a communist. Neither was he part of any political party or any movement. The government ensured that it continued to portray Chaplin in a negative way. Very soon, a demand was made stating, "He is not good for the country. We must chase him away!"

Two important people were against Chaplin in this regard. It was the previous FBI leader, Edgar Hoover and Joseph McCarthy. The latter was leading the team that was involved in finding those individuals and groups that worked against the country.

It affected the physical and mental health of Chaplin. Once, the Americans were fond of Chaplin and the scenario turned upside down. Unfortunately, well-planned fake allegations can destroy the goodwill of any individual.

The subsequent movies did not have quite an opening like his previous movies. Whenever his movies were released, people called for strikes, opposed the release, or formed protest processions. So, the theatre owners had an extreme fear of damage to their property and showed their disinterest towards releasing Chaplin's movies.

On August 1952. Chaplin went on a family tour to England to release his movie, which was not received well in the US. The minute he travelled out of the country in a ship, his rivals planned and acted upon it quickly. They created plots to keep him away from the US.

On August 1952. Chaplin went on a family tour to England to release his movie, which was not received well in the US. The minute he travelled out of the country in a ship, his rivals planned and acted upon it quickly. They created plots to keep him away from the US.

Two days after his departure, he was telegrammed. 'If you want to come back to the US, you must meet an investigation team. You will be permitted to enter the country only if your answers are satisfactory.'

It literally meant, 'do not ever think about coming back to the country'. Of course, the hidden message clearly indicated that he was not permitted to enter the country.

After that, what happened to Chaplin was not important. We must understand that the term 'communist' just made the FBI go crazy. FBI desperately wanted to chase away all those suspected as communists.

Indeed, both the US and Russia sailed in the same boat during the war. However, it transformed post-war.

After the end of the First World War, Russia was not honoured in global politics. In fact, every country said that

Russia was communist and wondered how it could affect them. No country had expected that Russia would develop as a significant country in the powerful global political arena.

Meanwhile, Soviet undercover agents had infiltrated the federal government, military and internal affairs. The major reason was, during the Second World War, both the countries considered Germany as their enemy. They were determined to go to any extent to defeat Hitler and his crew.

In the next twenty five years, Lenin, Stalin, and other leaders used the enormous human resources of Russia and quickly developed the country to another level. Everyone was shocked and equally surprised that the Soviet Union had captured a large chunk of space on the world map. The strength of the Soviet Union earned respect as well as fear.

The victories of Russia aka the Soviet Union during the Second World War substantially increased their strength. Russia had outgrown other countries in every aspect and easily competed with the superpower of America.

It was too late when the US realised this fact. Meanwhile, Soviet undercover agents had infiltrated the federal government, military and internal affairs.

The major reason was, during the Second World War, both the countries considered Germany as their enemy. They were determined to go to any extent to defeat Hitler and his crew. This made the US fail to realise whether the countries that offered help had any friendly intentions. While the US was happy with the destruction of the Nazi army, they recognised it rather late that in all offices, Russians and their allies held important positions.

This was not a major setback while the Soviet Union and the US were friendly to each other. When the Cold War began, the troubles began too.

When compared to the US, Soviet Union was far behind in some aspects and had the upper hand in some aspects. The US was stunned by this realisation. *What will happen if the Soviet Union steals our secrets? They could easily use their human resources and develop beyond expectations. We could land in big trouble.* Compared to Germany, Italy and Japan, the US realised that Russia was a bigger enemy. Immediately, their concerns about security and protection diverted to Russia.

In September 1947, the CIA—Central Intelligence Agency was formed to take care of the external affairs of America. They managed and controlled the violations that happened inside the boundaries of the Soviet Union against America. FBI handled the internal affairs and the undercover agents from the Soviet Union. The US followed the same tactics that the country followed during the world war. However, now their target wasn't Germany or Italy. The US did not want the Soviet Union to become a superpower and made plans to control the growth of the Soviet Union. Was that possible?

❑

8
Nuclear Bomb, Weapon and Danger

In the year 1944, the Second World War had not ended. During that period, the FBI carefully listened to all incoming and outgoing radio bulletins in the US. When they found any relevant information, the FBI informed the government and the army. One day, suddenly, some secret messages were sent to the Soviet Union from their embassy in New York. The FBI recorded it. Despite repeated efforts. they could not understand it .

The messages appeared bizarre and were probably coded. They could not understand it. However, the Bureau had sign language experts and a special department. The skilled experts of this section could easily crack open even the difficult symbolic languages. Unfortunately, even they could not decipher the Soviet sign language. Despite many efforts, they could not find the meaning of the words. All their efforts turned useless, the Bureau experts became frustrated.

They thought, “The Soviet Union is our friendly ally. Why should we read their secret message? Let’s focus on Hitler.”

After the end of the world war, the threat from the Nazi army came to an end. Subsequently, the Soviet Union threat began. The Bureau suspected whether the Soviets would steal their secrets or spy on them. Now, they suddenly remembered the old radio messages. They again started to decode the message.

After the end of the world war, the threat from the Nazi army came to an end. Subsequently, the Soviet Union threat began. The Bureau suspected whether the Soviets would steal their secrets or spy on them. Now, they suddenly remembered the old radio messages. They again started to decode the message.

At the same time, the US Army and other sections were hunting for the medicine to cure the Soviet threat. A spy agency called the ‘Army Security Agency’ conducted a lot of research and found a way to decode the secret messages of the Soviet Union. When the FBI heard about this, it started translating all their old messages to find any clues or any information about the Soviet agents.

The shocking news was revealed after two years. The translated messages came into the limelight. ‘Soviet Union has received the secret information about US nuclear bomb research.'

The two nuclear bombs that destroyed Japan towards the end of the world war were an outcome of their years of research. The world directly witnessed the extent of danger and irreversible damage caused by the bombs. So, the US decided to secure all the details about their research. If anyone else got the information, they could easily create a nuclear bomb. It could be a threat to the US. So, the country decided to conceal all information about the nuclear bomb from the Soviet Union. It was up to their scientists and researchers to create their own bombs. However, that could consume many years. Meanwhile, the US would have advanced in this research.

Of course, the US encountered the biggest blow to their plans. Already, the secrets of the nuclear bomb had leaked to the Soviet Union, a couple of years ago. The world was aware how swift the Russian scientists were. If they had received the secret messages, they might already have started creating the nuclear bomb.

In fact, whatever they suspected was true. In September 1949, the Soviet Union tested their first nuclear bomb. Within four years of the Hiroshima and Nagasaki bomb blast, the Soviets came up with a nuclear bomb. The major reason is that they got hold of the information about the American nuclear bomb research.

It doesn't mean that the Soviet Union was not talented enough to create their own nuclear bombs. They might have spent around seven to eightyears in creating the nuclear bomb.

However, someone had easily helped them to get the secrets from the US. Eventually, their research ended in a shorter time frame.

Who was the black sheep? Or the flock of sheep? The Bureau started their hunt. They clearly identified a fact that it has been passed via the Russian embassy. 'Project Manhattan' was the name of the American Nuclear Bomb Research teamwork. Those who were directly involved in this research had leaked and sold the information about the details of research, designs, and some important documents. A husband and wife were suspected of this crime. Unless the FBI caught them, they could not prevent the further leak of secrets.

The Bureau started their hunt. They clearly identified a fact that it has been passed via the Russian embassy. 'Project Manhattan' was the name of the American Nuclear Bomb Research teamwork. Those who were directly involved in this research had leaked and sold the information about the details of research, designs, and some important documents.

The Bureau started to investigate the suspected list of communists and evaluated whether anyone was involved in the Manhattan research. After a prolonged search, suspects, explanations, and validations, all of them pointed to a person—Glass Fasch.

Glass Fasch was born in Germany. However, during the early 30s, he escaped to England and settled there. He was one of the foreign experts when the US started its nuclear bomb research.

Many messages delivered to the Soviet Union indicated Glass Fasch. The FBI were sure that a direct interrogation could provide more details. However, they had a major problem. After the end of the Second World War, Glass Fasch moved back to England. It was impossible to bring him back to the country for inquiry.

In the beginning, Great Britain did not consider the request of the Bureau. Who would consider a random call without any proof? Britain was not ready to arrest or make enquiries about their citizens, blindly trusting the Bureau. The FBI understood this.

So what? England is our acquaintance. Even they are discontent with the Soviet Union. Won't they conduct an inquiry if we send them a message stating that he is suspected to be a communist spy?

The Bureau immediately contacted British intelligence. "You have a man named Glass Fasch. We suspect him to be a Soviet agent. Ensure that he doesn't escape. We are coming."

In the beginning, Great Britain did not consider the request of the Bureau. Who would consider a random call without any proof? Britain was not ready to arrest or make enquiries about their citizens, blindly trusting the Bureau. The FBI understood this. They explained what they had found about Glass Fasch. They made Britain understand that if Britain delayed, Glass Fasch would run away to the Soviet Union.

Britain understood the FBI's concern. They arrested Glass Fasch and started their interrogation. Later, the FBI also took part in this inquiry.

In the beginning, Glass Fasch did not cooperate. Later, he opened his mouth. He agreed that he sold many secrets about the research when he was working in Project Manhattan in New York and New Mexico.

This Harry Gold was a member of the American Communist Party. He was working in Philadelphia. When the suspect was proven, immediately, the FBI arrested him. He finally agreed that he had committed the crime, saying "I was the one who collected the secrets from Glass Fasch and delivered it to the Soviet Union!"

"OK. Who was your buyer?"

"Raymond!"

"Who's that?"

"I do not know his real name. Every time, he collected the information from me and would pay for that. Apart from this, I had no contact with any other Soviet Union members directly."

When the Bureau understood that Glass Fasch was telling the truth, they were disappointed. We thought of him as the leader of the criminals. What a joke, he was like an assistant! After that, the FBI found Glass Fasch to be of no use. They collected the information about Raymond and left the country.

In 1950, Glass Fasch was proven guilty of his crimes. The British court sentenced him to imprisonment of fourteen years.

At the same time, the FBI in the US actively engaged in finding the identity of Raymond. After a hell of an effort, finally, they found the real identity of Raymond. His real name was Harry Gold.

This Harry Gold was a member of the American Communist Party. He was working in Philadelphia. When the suspect was proven, immediately, the FBI arrested him. He finally agreed that he had committed the crime, saying "I was the one who collected the secrets from Glass Fasch and delivered it to the Soviet Union!"

"Is there anyone else who passed on the research secrets?"

"Yes. There is another person!"

The FBI was stunned. "Who's that?"

Harry Gold told, "He was working in Los Alamos. He belongs to the US Army I guess."

"His name?"

"I don't know. I met him in New Mexico. I gave him five hundred dollars and purchased a few secret documents."

"Will you be able to identify him through photos?"

"Sure!"

Then? The FBI showed the pictures from their suspected lists. Harry Gold picked a picture and said, "This is him."

The man Harry Gold identified was David Greenglass. On 16th June 1950, the FBI arrested him and started an inquiry about selling the nuclear bomb research secrets.

David Greenglass agreed to his crime. At the same time, he bargained. "If you give an assurance that I won't be punished severely, I'll reveal the name of another person involved."

The case still remained open despite Glass Fasch, Harry Gold and David Greenglass getting arrested. The FBI couldn't trace others. To get more information about them, the FBI agreed to David Greenglass' deal.

"It was my brother-in-law who lured me into snatching and selling the secrets of nuclear bombs to the Soviet Union for big money. His name is Julius Rosenberg."

Throughout the day, the Bureau interrogated Julius. However, he did not give in. He persistently said, "I don't know anything about America's nuclear bomb research. I came to know about the nuclear bombs only when Hiroshima and Nagasaki were destroyed."

The next morning, the Bureau knocked at Julius's door. "We want you for an inquiry. Come with us."

Throughout the day, the Bureau interrogated Julius. However, he did not give in. He persistently said, "I don't know anything about America's nuclear bomb research. I came to know about the nuclear bombs only when Hiroshima and Nagasaki were destroyed."

The FBI did not believe him. When they intensified their questioning, he became silent. "I will not speak a word without my attorney."

The Bureau again went back to David Greenglass. They tried to collect information that could lead to the arrest of Julius. After recording his words, they again went to Julius's residence. This time, it was not merely an inquiry. In 17 th July 1950 he was arrested as a suspect They started interrogating him more intensely than before. Still, he did not speak a word. He continued to say, "I don't know anything."

Julius had supported the communist party since his college days. He strongly believed that only socialism can reform the country and develop a society with no highs and lows. Yet, we cannot conclude that a man who supports communists or a member of a communist group is a spy of the Soviet Union. Either he must agree to his crimes or we need conclusive evidence without a shadow of a doubt.

It was not easy for the FBI to prove the crimes of the Rosenberg couple. Despite all efforts, they repeatedly said, "We are innocent. We did not do anything wrong."

Despite many efforts, the Bureau could not collect any proof of evidence against Julius. They were unable to prove Julius guilty of crimes merely based on the confessions of David Greenglass. When David Greenglass communicated with the FBI, he casually let out some information. "Whenever I speak to Julius, his wife Ethel would accompany him and make notes."

Now, the Bureau had a breakthrough. They planned to interrogate Ethel, collect the confession, and arrest Julius. Ethel was the sister of David Greenglass. So, based on his statement, on 11th August 1950 the Bureau arrested Ethel .

After that, the FBI agents grilled Julius Rosenberg and Ethel Rosenberg in many ways. A man named Sobell, who belonged to this group and also a Soviet supporter was arrested and questioned.

It was not easy for the FBI to prove the crimes of the Rosenberg couple. Despite all efforts, they repeatedly said, "We are innocent. We did not do anything wrong."

The FBI did not believe them. Based on the confessions by Harry Gold and David Greenglass, they collected many evidences, witnesses and filed a case against Julius, Ethel and Sobell. The court proceedings began on 6th March 1951.

The secret legal proceedings were exposed. Everyone came forward and confessed against Julius and Ethel. The case was filed because they had created a spy group to collect US nuclear bomb research secrets.

Even at that time, Mr. and Mrs. Rosenberg proclaimed their innocence. "We deny all these allegations. Everyone is trying to plot against us."

"Let the others be. David is your blood relative. What is the necessity for him to talk against you?"

"We were doing a business together. Unfortunately, we faced a loss. He was angry with us since then. He is trying to take revenge now," said Julius Rosenberg. "Besides, if he shows up as a witness against us, his sentence would be reduced. So, he decided to ruin the lives of his own sister and her husband."

"Let it go. Was it true that you were an undercover agent for the Soviet Union?

"Definitely, a big no!"

"Are you a communist?"

"I do not want to answer this question."

"Why?"

"If I say I am a communist, it could turn against me," said Julius. His wife also mirrored him. However, the court disagreed with them. Mr. and Mrs. Rosenberg were communist supporters even before they were married. A lot of witnesses were provided as proof of evidence. Meanwhile, Julius also made a big mistake. During the Second World War, he had developed sympathy for Russia and he accepted this in the court. Of course, he was true and fair in his statement.

Mr. and Mrs. Rosenberg were communist supporters even before they were married. A lot of witnesses were provided as proof of evidence. Meanwhile, Julius also made a big mistake. During the Second World War, he had developed sympathy for Russia and he accepted this in the court.

"I am a Jew. Russia battled against the Hitler army that killed lakhs of Jews. So, I developed an emotional bond with Russia."

Unfortunately, the court did not look at it fairly. They just perceived him as a communist. They concluded on a decision based on the witnesses and evidence provided by the FBI.

Till the end, the couple believed that the witnesses would be weak or insufficient. However, the judgement was contradictory to their belief on 29th March 1951. "The court has arrived at a decision that Julius Rosenberg, Ethel Rosenberg and Morton Sobell have been proven guilty of stealing the nuclear bomb research secrets."

Harry Gold was already sentenced to thirty years in jail term. Morton Sobell also had the same jail term. David Greenglass who gave information in favour of the Bureau received fifteen years of jail term. Mr. and Mrs. Rosenberg were issued the death penalty for directing all of them in this crime.

In the beginning, the FBI arrested Ethel to make Julius speak. However, both of them got capital punishment. In the history of America, no one was issued capital punishment for this kind of crime during the war-free era. So, many doubted whether the court of law was fair in issuing the death penalty to the couple.

> *The president during that period, Herbert Hoover explicitly stated, "Do not underestimate the crimes they did. They have laid a foundation for a nuclear war, which may affect millions of people. When we consider it from that viewpoint, it is unfair to forgive them."*

In the beginning, they claimed that the witnesses were not strong against the couple. "What did the Bureau prove? The couple was a communist. Was it even fair to give a death penalty based on that information and witnesses of fellow undercover agents? Tomorrow, my neighbour may file serious allegations against me. Based on that, am I guilty? Would I be killed sitting in an electric chair?" Many just boiled over the judgement.

Were the Rosenberg couple criminals? Or was it similar to Charlie Chaplin's case? Were they really innocents? Punished due to circumstances?

Based on these questions, throughout the US, riots erupted. Some claimed that since Julius was a Jew, this case just showed discrimination against him. Many demanded reopening of the case and reassessment of the punishment.

Neither the Bureau nor the federal government approved it. The president during that period, Herbert Hoover explicitly stated, "Do not underestimate the crimes they did. They have laid a foundation for a nuclear war, which may affect millions of people. When we consider it from that viewpoint, it is unfair to forgive them."

Just imagine that Julius was wrong. Why the death penalty for Ethel? For helping him? Could they not reduce the sentence considering that she was a woman?

"Never,said the government. "If we forgive Ethel now, tomorrow all countries will use female undercover agents."

In the next few months, the Rosenberg couple tried to appeal in many ways. All their friends and well-wishers tried to help them. Nothing worked.

In June 1953, the death penalty to Julius and Ethel was assured. As a last resort, the federal government lured them stating, "Agree to your crimes. Show us who your partners were. We could consider reducing your punishment."

Mr. and Mrs. Rosenberg denied it. "It proves that we are innocent. We will not admit to the crimes we did not commit."

The government believed they would change their mind till the last minute. It did not happen. On 19th June, both Julius and Ethel died on the electric chair. Even after the death of the couple, many people rallied claiming they were innocents. Most importantly, their friends and children persistently claimed it. For many years, they were believed to be innocent.

After many years, many secret documents of the Russian Intelligence, KGB were leaked via Vasili Mitrokhin. The continuous help provided by Mr. and Mrs. Rosenberg was mentioned. It seems that the couple had played a pivotal role in speeding up Soviet Union's nuclear bomb research. Not just nuclear bombs, but the Soviet Union was keen to gather all information about every move of the US. Whether they used it or not, they wanted to keep themselves updated about their rival country.

So, for the next forty years, there was no shortage of Soviet undercover agents in the US. When someone went, another person arrived. In some or the other way, the Soviet Union continued to receive information. The FBI was fully engaged in dealing with them.

❑

9
True or False

In olden days when kings invaded a country, their forces would take away all the gold, silver, diamonds and precious gems of the vanquished country. Some people would chase and abduct women. They occupied homes and shops. This is usually the case even now though the algorithms have changed slightly since then.

Another new things was added to this list in the early part of the last century. The troops victorious in the war entering a country began not just to take away cash and other valuables but also the official documents available there.

What will they do with the documents?

A lot can be done. A good example is the life of William Fischer.

> *The following year, the Second World War began. It took a lot of effort to train many of the spies and radio operators who were infiltrating the German frontier. He was again recruited by the Soviet Army. It was during this period that he began associating with several spies.*

British-born William Fischer's parents were from Russia. During the reign of the Tsars, they were a part of the rebellious forces that opposed it. Unfortunately, during their time there was not enough public support for these riots. The government crushed them. They fled from Russia in 1900 and settled in England. Two years later they had a son, William Fischer. When he was fourteen, the Tsar's regime in Russia was overthrown.

After that, William's family was not restrained from returning to Russia. In 1912, eighteen years old,William settled in Moscow.

William was fluent in both English and Russian. So, he worked as a translator for a few years. He then joined the army and also trained as a radio operator. For the next ten years, he held several minor responsibilities in the Soviet Army. He also served as head of a training school for radio operators at one point. Yet, the Soviet superiors did not have full confidence in him. They were reluctant to hand over to him any highly secretive work because he was born in England. In 1938, due to some problems he was fired from his job.

The following year, the Second World War began. It took a lot of effort to train many of the spies and radio operators who were infiltrating the German frontier. He was again recruited by the Soviet Army. It was during this period that he began associating with several spies. He learnt many things, such as gathering information without anyone suspecting him and sending it to the Soviet government.

> *So, if the Soviet agents go to the US, they work very carefully so that the Bureau will not be able to trace their Soviet background in any way as a variety of fake documents would be prepared for it. They would make sure that the FBI couldn't trace the origin of the Soviet intruder into the US.*

The US became the prime rival of the Soviet Union after the Second World War. Many of their agents came and lived here under pseudonyms. They did random jobs; they looked after the work of gathering information here, looking for people to execute the secret tasks, selecting people to help them, making money, sending that information secretly, and so on.

It was at this point that William was chosen. There were two main reasons for this. He was fluent in English and had natural Western habits. So, no one would doubt him. Once it was decided to send him to the US, a large group began to work on it. Their job was to find a way to get him to the US.

Isn't there a simple flight ticket that can take you straight and land in the US?The answer is NO.

If someone from the Soviet Union comes to the US, there were thousands of rules and regulations to comply. Questions, suspicions, inquiries and more. If they had any doubts about William, he would be sent back straight away. Based on the information like, were his parents native to Russia, whether he served in the Russian military, or worked in different government departments, he would be easily stamped as a suspect. It held a big risk. So, if the Soviet agents go to the US, they work very carefully so that the Bureau will not be able to trace their Soviet background in any way as a variety of fake documents would be prepared for it. They would make sure that the FBI couldn't trace the origin of the Soviet intruder into the US.

The restrictions were not just limited to the Soviet Union. The intelligence department of all the countries have an exclusive department for 'special documents'. The objective of the department is to create the documents for people who travel abroad. At this juncture, the documents related to foreign theft helped. For instance, let's see what happened to William Fischer.

In 1984, William Fischer went to the US. However, he used the passport of Andrew Kayotis.

Who was Andrew Kayotis?

Andrew kayotis was born and brought up in the US. He died when he was in Lithuania during 1947. Soviet Union caught hold of the passport of the deceased Andrew. They used that passport and disguised William Fischer, and sent him to Canada. After spending months in Canada, Fischer went to New York as Andrew Kayotis. It may have happened around 1950.

Immediately after entering the US, he was named as 'Emil Goldfus' and the names were changed in the documents. Emil was born in New York. Both were of similar age with a difference of onlyfew months. However, Emil Goldfus died even before he turned one and a half years.

Soviet intelligence somehow collected information about the Emil Goldfus who died 47 years ago. They altered everything and handed it over to William Fischer. Despite the meticulous efforts in preparing flawless documentation, Soviet officers were afraid. They decided that Fischer should not work anywhere in the US and must own his business.

A comprehensive background information would be conducted when someone is employed in the US companies. So, their history must be neat and clean. Keep aside the employment. If anyone informed the police or the FBI and if they got suspicious of William Fisher, it would be the end of the story. So, the Soviet Union decided not to take any risks.

❑

10
Before and After Hoover

When you hear the word 'spy', you would imagine a vibrant young man. who will run faster than other normal people. His brain works many times faster than normal people. If an undercover agent is like this, imagine what it would be like to be the leader of several hundred to several thousand agents. You consider him not lesser than Superman.

It is this imaginary picturisation that has caused irritation and frustration to the FBI in the 60s. The FBI leader Hoover, did not fit in at all with the idea created by many crime novels and the Hollywood movies and agents.

No offence,It is unreasonable to expect him to work like a James Bond and deal with teasing at his age. What a wonderful way to screw people over and get their day started with the seventyyearsold senior citizen as the FBI's leader. How long would it take to send him home and find some eligible candidate as the leader of FBI?

In the late 60s, Edgar's old-fashioned management and actions came under heavy criticism. Many lamented that the Soviet Union and others would defeat them if they continued using ancient techniques without understanding the advancements. The FBI began to voice its support for modernization.

The US government could not do that either. Hoover had been the pillar to the FBI who had built a treasure trove for over forty years, and he would get angry if the government talked about retirement. It was also probably not a good idea to anger someone who knows all the secrets of the nation. So, they had no choice. The FBI kept him in power.

In the late 60s, Edgar's old-fashioned management and actions came under heavy criticism. Many lamented that the Soviet Union and others would defeat them if they continued using ancient techniques without understanding the advancements. The FBI began to voice its support for modernization.

All this time, they also had been very careful throughout the tenure to bring the latest technology to the FBI. Yet, most commented that it was not enough. Edgar died on 2nd May 1972. He was the head of the FBI for almost forty eight years.

Following Edgar's death, the Bureau appointed an interim director. His name was Patrick Gray. Exactly six weeks later, just after midnight on 16th June 1972, some burglars broke into a Watergate hotel in Washington. This hotel has now become very popular across the world.At that time ‘Richard Nixon’ was the president of the US . One of his opposition, the Democratic Party offices was located inside the Watergate Hotel.

The thieves had just entered the party office. They were fixing tapping devices in several places. Fortunately, one of the night guards noticed the open door. They were trapped easily with electronic equipment.

Who would benefit from tapping the Democratic Party activities? Does it benefit the ruling party? That’s where the media struck gold. Gordon Liddy was a part of the planning committee set up by Nixon for the 1972 election.

Initially, many people thought that these five people planned to steal something from the office. Upon background investigation, it was revealed that there was a powerful person behind this plan. The name of that great storm was Garden Liddy, a former FBI officer.

What a new problem is this? When someone who did once worked for the FBI ,form a thieving gang privately? Or there was someone else involved? Then FBI very eagerly began to dig into Garden’s background.

When they broke into the Watergate Hotel, they stole nothing. The police found the tapping device and they were caught. *Who would benefit from tapping the Democratic Party activities? Does it benefit the ruling party?*

That’s where the media struck gold. Gordon Liddy was a part of the planning committee set up by Nixon for the 1972 election.

What does that mean? Was this man using all the intricacies of the relationship he learnt in the FBI to spy on Nixon's enemies now? Another important question! Did the leader have the permission for these actions or was this person acting arbitrarily? From the beginning, Nixon denied that he had anything to do with the incidents. The people voted for him and elected him president again.

The US media, which never had any of these problems, were exposing a number of issues that were still not resolved. President Nixon created a serious political crisis. In fact, the FBI should have cleared up the issue. That did not happen and there was a suspicion that perhaps they were deliberately going slow on Nixon's command.

Later, the incidents became even bigger, The court confirmed Gordon's crimes in the Watergate incident. During the ensuing interrogation, voices began to be heard calling for his resignation. Gordon Liddy Left with no choice, he served his resignation notice and disappeared from public life.

At the same time, the victim of the hotel Watergate affair was not only Nixon but also the honour and the respect of the FBI. For a long time, it was FBI's tradition to investigate if any major problem arose in the limits of the US borders. Even when President 'John F Kennedy' was assassinated in November 1963, the new President 'Lindon Johnson' called the FBI and handed over the case.

According to the existing practices, the FBI was given the responsibility of investigating the hotel Watergate incident. They were fully qualified and capable of it. However, the FBI agents from the beginning could not properly investigate the case. Many kinds of political obstacles, crises and problems were dragging them back from letting them run freely.

The US media, which never had any of these problems, were exposing a number of issues that were still not resolved. President Nixon created a serious political crisis. In fact, the FBI should have cleared up the issue. That did not happen and there was a suspicion that perhaps they were deliberately going slow on Nixon's command. There were even critics who had questioned the FBI's performance on a number of issues before.

For the first time now, their integrity was in question. Many questioned whether an intelligence agency that would investigate any case impartially and reveal the truth could go so far as to pull the strings of the government. No one was able to confirm their suspicions; everything still remained a mystery.

There were two important journalists who shot to prominence during the Watergate incident—Bob Woodward and Carl Bernstein. Both were reporters at *The Washington Post.* These two journalists were the only ones who were constantly getting important news on the Watergate case. No one had any idea as to who gave all this information and how it is delivered.

Shortly after Nixon resigned, the two journalists co-authored a book on the Watergate affair. It was the first time they had mentioned the secret man who had given them information.

A man nick named 'Deep Throat', held a responsible position in the federal government. So, he had friends at all levels that could not be easily accessed by journalists. Unbeknownst to him, he leaked details of the Watergate affair to '*The Washington Post'* journalists, which he thought would be suppressed by the US government.

Thus, the pressure was put on the FBI from the White House throughout the Watergate investigation and finally came in to the limelight as a crisis. Patrick Gray, the then interim director of the FBI, also revealed that he had deliberately suppressed the investigation. Patrick Gray who resigned on 23rd April 1933, was replaced by Clarence Kelly.

The first challenge faced by Clarence Kelly after he took charge as a chairman was to fix the damaged FBI reputation destroyed in the hotel Watergate case and to impart public confidence again.

The identity of 'Deep Throat' was not revealed until 2005. Everyone had a hearty and meaningful laugh when they found out it was Mark Felt. Although the FBI slipped, it was indeed a proud moment that it was another FBI agent who unlocked the mystery.

For the next several months, he worked very hard and completed all his tasks. As the Bureau underwent various changes during this period, gradually people began to forget the damaged reputation. The Bureau gained the old respect.

Who is 'Deep Throat' who nailed Nixon and the Bureau director at the same time? He was also an FBI agent and its associate director, Mark Felt.

The identity of 'Deep Throat' was not revealed until 2005. Everyone had a hearty and meaningful laugh when they found out it was Mark Felt. Although the FBI slipped, it was indeed a proud moment that it was another FBI agent who unlocked the mystery.

There is one more,Though the FBI had an ugly role model in its history of Watergate incident, they never tried to cover it up and rewrite it. During the centenary celebrations in 2008, they published an official handbook on the Watergate investigations, which described the disruptions, corruptions and the resignation of the director.

The FBI had to face even bigger threats in the next ten years after the Watergate investigation. From local riots to the external forces that infiltrated the US, there was a lot to encounter.

> *Terrorist threats were high not only in the US but around the world in the late 1970s. Different movements put forward different demands and staged direct attacks on their own or foreign governments. A bomber once struck in front of a crowd of protesters. Bombings occurred in all places from hotels to theatres to airports to government offices and embassies.*

Thus, the FBI had to upgrade itself with urgency. From improving the personal performance of agents to weapons to laboratories and ancillary equipment with modern technology, everything was more advanced than ever before.

The effects of these changes became apparent immediately in the seven years from 1981 to 1987, when the FBI captured and imprisoned more than a thousand mafia leaders and their group. The FBI destroyed the mafia influence that was causing anarchy in many cities of the US.

Terrorist threats were high not only in the US but around the world in the late 1970s. Different movements put forward different demands and staged direct attacks on their own or foreign governments. A bomber once struck in front of a crowd of protesters. Bombings occurred in all places from hotels to theatres to airports to government offices and embassies.

As such riots began to take place within the US from time to time, the press and the public began to ask a question. *Whose responsibility is it to prevent all this? Police? Army? Security Force? FBI? Or should we put the burden on the Almighty?*

In fact, there was no strong organisation in place to prevent such attacks within the US. The army could not be brought in at any cost. At the same time, they needed to find a way between the two if they had to rely solely on routine police action to prevent terrorist activities.

The US government was thinking that the 1984 Olympics was approaching and it was scheduled to take place in Los Angeles. It was a great honour to host the internationally acclaimed Olympics. But athletes from many countries would arrive at the US. Fans who visited the country to watch their favourites play would be greeted by a large crowd of tourists. *How to ensure safety in the midst of the crowd? What if any extremist organisation that is angry with the US, infiltrates the Olympics and causes chaos?*

The US had reasons to fear. At the 1972 Munich Olympics, a militant group entered and hunted down Israeli athletes. How would you make sure no such fuss would happen in Los Angeles?

After brainstorming, the US government came to a conclusion,they created a separate unit called the HRT—

'Hostage Rescue Team' and handed it over to the FBI. The purpose of this HRT department was to monitor issues related to the unit. To deal with a situation where someone was holding someone hostage and handle them.

Created in 1982, the first goal of the department was to ensure that there were no problems at the Los Angeles Olympics. They did not let that unit dissolve immediately after its success. Similar situations might appear in the future. So, they announced that the unit would continue to operate.

Sophisticated weapons gave them ability to cope with any situation with the help of electronic devices. It was around this time that the group began to develop sophisticated members who worked without knives or guns. The FBI was preparing itself to detect the latest corruption scandals.

Over the next quarter-century, the department had undergone various changes and improvements. Their style was to infiltrate the other side while the police or other officers were talking to them and bring the situation under control.

The officers of this HRT unit were trained in everything from helicopter to boat rides. Sophisticated weapons gave them ability to cope with any situation with the help of electronic devices. It was around this time that the group began to develop sophisticated members who worked without knives or guns. The FBI was preparing itself to detect the latest corruption scandals.

To manage them, the entire Bureau was computerised. Subsidiaries such as the Computer Analysis and Response

Team, also known as the CART, were created. A special unit for detecting computer-related crimes called Cyber Division was also set up during this period.

Another face of viciousness came out. Both men were perverted paedophiles. That's why they lured the children using sweets and candy. Many of the children who had lived in the area for years had fallen prey to them. Something even worse happened. They also filmed the perverted scenes and broadcast them on the internet.

The impact of the computers and the internet was growing not only in the US but also around the world. So, many new problems had sprouted. For example, in May 1993, a little boy from Maryland, Brentwood of the US suddenly disappeared.

Th local police and some FBI agents raided every home to search for the tenyearsold boy. They tried to find out where the little boy was, but to no avail. However, what some boys and girls told their investigators later shocked the FBI. "There was a neighbour. He would buy young boys food, clothes, give them money and take them on trips." FBI guessed that there must be some devious reason for him to get closer to the boys. Another man was also suspected.

Immediately the agents began to monitor the two men. Every day, all the details were collected: where they were going, who they were seeing, and what they were talking about etc., were prepared and mailed to their superiors. On the other hand, the FBI had also stepped up investigations to find out their background.

Soon their masks were torn. Another face of viciousness came out. Both men were perverted paedophiles. That's why they lured the children using sweets and candy. Many of the children who had lived in the area for years had fallen prey to them.

Something even worse happened. They also filmed the perverted scenes and broadcast them on the internet. People with similar disgusting thoughts around the world were found enjoying watching them and writing ugly comments.

Normally, FBI agents are said to be very brave. However, they themselves were extremely shocked to see these photos and videos. *Were there really such horrible people in the world? What would happen if the public watched these videos?*

It had started as a normal kidnapping case and the FBI had become a very important part of it because of the intensity of the case. *Who was exploiting children for sexual purposes across the US? What kind of methods do they follow to kidnap children? What is their network like? Do the children understand what happens to them? Do they convey anything about this to their parents or friends or teachers? How would they be affected in the future?* Many more agents came out to continue the investigation from this angle.

In 1994-95, the FBI launched a separate unit called Innocent Images. Its purpose was to protect American children from such perverts, and educate parents to protect their children from being trapped by anyone like this, and also bringing the perpetrators to justice and punishing them.

When the FBI first talked about it, most members of the public could not even believe it. After investigating more than

100 homes and proving the crimes with evidence, they were shocked to realise how dangerous the situation was in which they were living.

What the perverts are unaware of is that everything they say is recorded on the FBI's computers so that they can easily find out who they are and where they are from. Maybe, they never thought they could get caught using a public computer.

In the following years, the FBI's Innocent Images expanded exponentially. Today, the internet in the US is under constant surveillance. The unit has arrested several thousand people for posting explicit photos and videos of children.

The methods used by agents are very interesting. They pose as children online and wait for someone to talk to them. They respond naively to comments and act as though they don't comprehend when the perverts talk inappropriately. When asked if they can meet in person, they would immediately say yes.

What the perverts are unaware of is that everything they say is recorded on the FBI's computers so that they can easily find out who they are and where they are from. Maybe, they never thought they could get caught using a public computer. Proving their guilt based on the evidence already recorded made conviction easier.

This is evidenced by the fact that till date, the number of cases reported by Innocent Images exclusively is closer to 30,000. The number of those arrested were about 10,000 from which more than seventy percent have been convicted.

Parents who have young children using the internet may want to read the FBI's handbook, and visit their website. There are so many types of risk on the internet and we know all too well how to protect our children from getting caught up in it.

That's right, what happened to that Maryland kid who was the reason behind saving thousands of kids? Did they find him or not? A search of the FBI's official history book revealed that they have no information about the whereabouts of the boy till now.

❑

11
Wall

It was on 26th February 1993, Mid-noon. A truck bomb was detonated below the North Tower of the World Trade Centre in New York.

Thousands were injured in the blast and six of them died. It came as more of a surprise than a shock to everyone, from the New York Police to the FBI.

The terrorist organisations that organised the bombing in New York had expected at least two and a half million heads to roll in it, but failed. The FBI agents undertook a massive manhunt.

The first clue came to the FBI, which carefully sifted through the wreckage. They found parts of a vehicle which had exploded from the inside out. They found a vehicle identification number and traced it to a van which had been stolen from a car rental agency in New Jersey. So, the person who rented the van or stole it from them must have belonged to a terrorist group. Agents flew to New Jersey to unravel this mystery.

Their luck was with a man who rented the van at a company called DIB Leasing in New Jersey. He was there to get back his four hundred dollars deposit money.

Mohammad Salameh was picked up by FBI agents and interrogated. With the assistance from Mohammad Salameh, they searched a co-conspirator's (Ramzi Yousuf) apartment where they found bomb-making material. By this time, Ramzi Yousuf had flown to Pakistan.

Mohammad Salameh was picked up by FBI agents and interrogated. With the assistance from Mohammad Salameh, they searched a co-conspirator's (Ramzi Yousuf) apartment where they found bomb-making material. By this time, Ramzi Yousuf had flown to Pakistan. In 1995, he was arrested by the Pakistani ISI and extradited to the US. He is currently in jail.

The US has faced a number of terrorist threats before and after the 1993 New York bombings. Attacks have also been carried out. The FBI was looking for a way to identify and suppress the terrorist groups. At the same time, the rise of the US on the inside has not diminished even in the slightest. However, the US made some mistakes and the adversaries took advantage of them.

CIA agents were very helpful in tracking down the suspects and arranging the necessary preventive measures. But let's assume that a person on this suspected list is coming into the

US. The CIA does not have the power to stop him. However, they can always inform the police that they should keep an eye on him, whether they follow it or not.

At the same time, many forces were gaining strength against the US. Essentially, Osama Bin Laden's Al-Qaeda movement. The terrorist groups also planned to bomb key landmarks. While thinking seriously about this, they came up with another new idea. What if instead of bombs, planes are used as weapons?

The CIA alone cannot be blamed for this. There has always been a power struggle among the security forces of almost all the US intelligence agencies. So, they were reluctant to give away the information for what they had worked so hard. Thus, having to do the same job over and over again, to derive almost identical information cost a lot of money.

Let the money go. What a security loophole it would be if a person on the CIA's list of suspects could easily enter the US because of an invisible wall between them.

This was the situation throughout the US in the 90s. What was worse, that no one in the US intelligence agency, the police, the military, the US Congress, the ministers or the president, realised that their stronghold had a weakness. No one even seemed to want to step up security at the border. Even though they wanted to prohibit entry to some, they had not thought about how to implement it.

For example, the Federal Aviation Administration (FAA) monitors aviation in the US. They have a list called 'No Fly'. The list has people who were not allowed to fly within US borders. In the 1990s, only twelve terrorists were on the list.

However, the number of suspects on the government list had exceeded thousands. Probably, not all government departments had a complete information about terrorists. In other words, they had not even fully realised the potential for harm to themselves by extremist organisations against the US. At the same time, many forces were gaining strength against the US. Essentially, Osama Bin Laden's Al-Qaeda movement. The terrorist groups also planned to bomb key landmarks. While thinking seriously about this, they came up with another new idea. What if instead of bombs, planes are used as weapons?

The plan was to hijack American planes and crash them into important buildings. Any building would be shattered if that happened. It was a strange weapon system that no one had thought of until then. The US security agencies were unlikely to anticipate this. Al-Qaeda's plan was kept a top secret. No one was told the full details of this except for a very few leaders. Even those who participated directly in these were confused as to exactly who their associates were, and what they were doing. The main purpose was to ensure that the US intelligence did not get any information about this in any way. Their slight alertness would make all efforts go in vain. Those who had to hijack and crash the plane would be unable to enter the US. Many Al-Qaeda fighters began arriving in the US in the early 2000s. Some of them and many of the other terror groups were on the suspect list, but no one here was blocking or tracking them. For the next several months, they learnt English in the US, got used to the culture, took flight lessons and here too, they had no problems.

The date for the attack was set for 11thSeptember . After that, they moved fast. Everything was perfectly planned, right from who was hijacking the aircraft to when and how to conceal their weapons. Tickets for that were purchased. What were the FBI agents doing when all this was going on across the US border? At first, even basic information about this was not available. So, they made no effort to track down these terrorists. According to US President 'George W Bush', the CIA had only received information that the terrorists might launch an attack on the US. The fact that Bin Laden was trying to attack the US was a secret known to all.

According to US President 'George W Bush', the CIA had only received information that the terrorists might launch an attack on the US. The fact that Bin Laden was trying to attack the US was a secret known to all.

Throughout 2001, the president received more than thirty informative notes about Al-Qaeda's attempts to attack the country. These failed to gain prominence among the other blue reports they sent.

On 6th August 2001, another report was sent to the CIA chief stating that Bin Laden was planning an attack inside the US border. Well, what was next? The chancellor went beyond that statement. The agency claimed that this was the thirty sixth report they sent in the year 2001 alone, in the case of Bin Laden.

The president was sharing some of the information they had gathered during the standoff with the Al-Qaeda militants who planned the hijacking. Why could the FBI not sniff out such a large gang planning to operate within the US border, let alone the CIA? Then what were they doing with thousands of agents? In fact, it was not until July 2001 that an FBI agent became suspicious. He noted that some Al-Qaeda militants seem to be joining American pilot training schools and learning to fly.

Four US planes were hijacked by Al-Qaeda militants. Two of them crashed into the Twin Towers in New York City. The third plane hit the Pentagon building, the majestic symbol of the US military. The fourth plane crashed into a field without reaching the target (probably the White House) the terrorists had planned.

What could be done with this information? A lot could be done by contacting all the pilot training institutes in the US at that time and collecting details of the new foreigners who had joined in the last twelve months and giving those names to the government to check if there were any suspicious persons who had enrolled as trainees. To investigate and confirm Al-Qaeda links, they should be investigated in this way. FBI could have acted in this case even without the help of CIA or other agencies. But they never bothered to do so and left it unattended.

On 4th September 2001, Robert Muller became the new director of the FBI. Exactly one week later, the attack shook the entire US. Four US planes were hijacked by Al-Qaeda militants. Two of them crashed into the Twin Towers in New York City. The third plane hit the Pentagon building, the majestic symbol of the US military. The fourth plane crashed into a field without reaching the target (probably the White House) the terrorists had planned. This attack, which claimed thousands of lives, was a great humiliation to the US. Both the CIA and FBI were responsible for this in some way. President 'George W Bush' spoke on American television within hours of the attack.

He declared war on terrorists. The same day in the evening, a council of commanders decided to support the president in this battle. The CBI Director George Bennett and FBI's new director, Robert Muller were also present. They decided that the perpetrators of these attacks must be identified as soon as possible. They must be arrested and punished regardless of whether they were inside or outside the US.

The punishment should be such that no one should even imagine such an attack in the future. All this must happen immediately. On the one hand, the US State Department report came down in support of the crisis in Pakistan, Afghanistan and other countries. On the other hand, FBI was given the responsibility of identifying local Al-Qaeda supporters or their fraternal organisations. This responsibility had remained with the FBI even before the 9/11 attack. But now there was a difference.

"All our agencies should work together and share their intelligence. No one anywhere in the world should even think of laying a finger against the US. We should do whatever it takes to do it." What President 'George W Bush' said about the war was not simply in the sense of lifting the gun. "The US military will take care of the fighting work. Everything else is the responsibility of the police and spy agencies."

'George W Bush' wanted to show how effective the spy agencies could be, if they forgot all internal politics during the war. Following this, the war against terrorism spread throughout the US. People began to view with suspicion, all foreigners, Muslims and non-English speakers. The US scrutinized everyone arriving and departing on international flights with a magnifying glass. No one could cross the US borders unless FBI showed the green flag. In six or seven more years, it was time for FBI to celebrate its centenary. They once again had to change their face completely differently.

❑

12
The Cat and Mouse Chase

The next day after the 9/11 attack, more than twenty five percent of the FBI agents were shifted to that single case. The primary objective was to find the terrorists involved in the act, and find the associates or group that helped them. At the same time, they also determined to identify whether similar attacks were planned.

On the day of the 9/11 attack, the Americans were disheartened when the terrorist flight attacked one of the Twin Towers. No one expected that another flight would attack the second tower.

When the first of the Twin Tower was attacked and started collapsing, civilians in the other Twin Tower were witnessing it, distressed over the attack and even pitying the victims of the attack. They never had a clue that they must run away to save their lives. While wondering about the attack, the flight hit and blew up the second tower, followed by the attack on the Pentagon. The second attack on the Twin Tower and the third on the Pentagon broke their fearless minds. Everyone shivered in fear imagining the attack of the fourth flight.

In continuation of these attacks, the US totally halted all air transport including commercial planes. However, they were unable to stop the rumours. A lot of imaginary stories popped up and spread all over the country about the upcoming terrorist attacks throughout the country.

In the entire history of the FBI, they had never spent so much resources in terms of money, time and manpower. They identified the terrorists associated with the 9/11 attack. They stabilised their connection or association with Al-Qaeda. Post ensuring the connections, together with CIA and other agencies, FBI collectively fastened the safety protocols.

If the government wanted to put an end to these rumoured stories, it must prove that the country was in safe hands with zero suspects in any confederacy. Eventually, the FBI was assigned this task.

In the entire history of the FBI, they had never spent so much resources in terms of money, time and manpower. They identified the terrorists associated with the 9/11 attack. They stabilised their connection or association with Al-Qaeda. Post ensuring the connections, together with CIA and other agencies, FBI collectively fastened the safety protocols.

In the next few weeks, the search for Bin Laden intensified. While FBI did not directly get involved in the hunt of Bin Laden, the agents ensured that Al-Qaeda could not plan any activity within the borders of the US.

Of course, the FBI was well informed that the impact of 9/11 might not subside anytime sooner. The director, Robert Muller realised that their primary responsibility was to ensure the safety and security protocols that destroyed terrorist groups.

The FBI director, Robert Muller, initiated another important episode in the history of the FBI, on 29th May 2002. The FBI created and released the list of top ten important responsibilities.

1. Secure and protect the country from terrorists attacks.
2. Ensure safety and protection to prevent or destroy the plans of the spy agencies from other countries.
3. Ensure cyber security to the country by harnessing the technological advancements.
4. Fight against corruption from lowest to the highest level of management.
5. Protect the rights of the civilians.
6. Identifying the criminal groups / setups that function at domestic and international level.
7. Control white collar crimes.
8. Support the domestic, national and international level security / intelligence agencies.
9. Control the violent activities.
10. Enhance and introduce the modern technologies to meet the goals and priorities of the FBI.

As expected, the priority was to eradicate terrorism. While the US had executed many plans and stunts to eradicate the Al-Qaeda and kill Osama Bin Laden post the 9/11 attack, what if someone could get the idea to hijack a passenger flight? Eventually, the new look of FBI gained higher importance among the civilians.

A week after the 9/11 attacks, letters containing anthrax spores were mailed to several people including senators and journalists. Of course, only after a few deaths, both the federal government and the FBI became cautious. They found the chain of link but not the source.

A week after the 9/11 attacks, letters containing anthrax spores were mailed to several people including senators and journalists. Of course, only after a few deaths, both the federal government and the FBI became cautious. They found the chain of link but not the source.

Recently, the FBI celebrated hundred years of service. With advanced technology and skilled agents, FBI tried to attack the new enemies. When their enemies tried new tactics, every time the FBI came up with new plans and methods to counter-attack. Of course, this was a very dangerous chase game.

The US never wanted to give up the 'number one' place to any other country or for any other reason. If the country wanted to retain the top position, the support of the intelligence agencies like FBI must be active 24/7. And the federal government was ready to provide any resources like manpower, technology, money, and literally anything to support the agents.

From this perception, we can conclude that their enemies controlled themselves and lay low. Did they advance in some other unanticipated ways? Could the FBI handle them? Did the FBI encounter a new set of rivals? Who knows!

❑

References

Books

- Athan G Theoharis, Tony G Poveda, Susan Rosenfeld, Richard Gid Power—*The FBI: A Comprehensive Reference Guide*. Checkmark Books, 2005
- Louis J Freeh—*My FBI*. St. Martin's Press, 2005
- Heather Lehr Wagner—*The Federal Bureau of Investigation*. Chelsea House Publishers,2007
- John J Miller and others—*The FBI: A Centennial History*
- *Federal Bureau of Investigation*—Faircount LLC, 2008
- Gail Karlitz—*FBI Agent*. Ferguson, 2009
- Bryan Burrough—*Public Enemies: America's Greatest Crime Wave and the Birth of the FBI*. Penguin Books, 2009
- John Douglas, Mark Olshaker—*Mindhunter*. Pocket Books, 1996
- Gary Aldrich—*Unlimited Access*. Regnery Publishing Inc., 1996

- John Douglas, Mark Olshaker—*Obsession*. Pocket Books, 1998
- Roger Boar, Nigel Blundell—*The World's Greatest Spies & Spymasters*. Octopus Books, 1985
- Christopher Andrew, Vasili Mitrokhin—*The Sword and the Shield: The Mitrokhin Archive and the Secret History of KGB*. Basic Books, 2001
- Glenn Hastedt—*Espionage: A Reference Handbook*. ABC-CLIO, 2003
- Editors: K Lee Lerner, Brenda Wilmoth—*Encyclopedia of Espionage, Intelligence and Security*. Thomson Gale, 2004
- Louis F Burns —*A History of the Osage People*. University of Alabama Press, 2004
- *The 9/11 Report - National Commission on Terrorist Attacks*. St. Martin's Paperbacks, 2004
- டாலர்தேசம்–பா. ராகவன் - கிழக்குபதிப்பகம், 2004
- Webster Griffin Tarpley—*9/11 Synthetic Terror*. Progressive Press, 2005
- Steven T Usdin—*Engineering Communism*. Yale University Press, 2005
- *The Secret Man: The Story of Watergate's Deep Throat*—Bob Woodward. Simon & Schuster, 2005
- Christopher M Finan—*From the Palmer Raids to the Patriot Act*. Beacon Press, 2007

Articles

- John F Fox—'The Birth of the Federal Bureau of Investigation Office of Public/Congressional Affairs'. Federal Bureau of Investigation, 2003
- John F Fox, Jnr.—'In the Enemy's House: Venona and the Maturation of American Counterintelligence'. Symposium on Cryptologic History, 2005
- John F Fox Jnr.—'Bureaucratic Wrangling over Counterintelligence, 1917–18'. Central Intelligence Agency, 2007
- Jon D May—'Osage Murders'. Oklahoma Historical Society

Websites

- http://www.fbi.gov/
- https://www.cia.gov/library/center-for-the-study-of-intelligence/csipublications/csistudies/studies/vol49no1/html_files/bureaucratic_wragling_2.html
- http://digital.library.okstate.edu/encyclopedia/entries/O/OS005.html
- http://trac.syr.edu/tracfbi/atwork/current/fbiHistory.html

Others

- Inside The FBI - National Geographic Channel, 2003
- FBI 100: A Closer Look (Radio Show) - Schiff & Fox, 2008

❑